The Journal of
Watkin Stench

The Journal of Watkin Stench

Meredith Hooper

Lutterworth Press
Cambridge

Lutterworth Press
P.O. Box 60
Cambridge CB1 2NT

British Library Cataloguing in Publication Data

Hooper, Meredith
The journal of Watkin Stench.
I. Title
823[J]

ISBN 0-7188-2756-2
ISBN 0-7188-2755-4 Pbk

Line drawings and cover illustration by Warron Prentice

First published 1988 by Lutterworth Press

Printed in Great Britain by
The Guernsey Press Co. Ltd.
Guernsey, Channel Islands

Watkin Stench

dedicates this Journal to his parents in London

and

Meredith Hooper

dedicates it to her parents in Australia

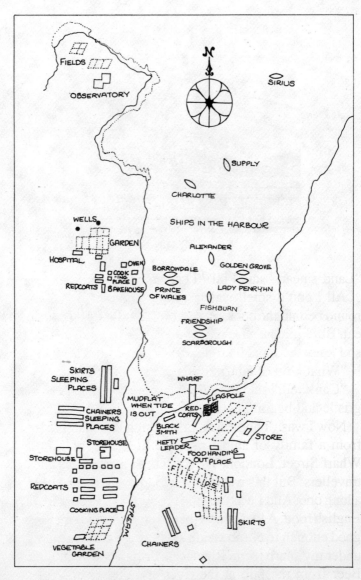

Sydney Cove, autumn 1788

1

"Land's near," said Phil. "I can smell it."

All I could smell was last night's dinner. We were round behind the cooking pots looking for something to eat. But Phil is a wise old rat and he has travelled a lot, so I knew he must be right.

"What kind of land?" I asked.

"Can't tell," said Phil, finding a bone with a piece of gristle and beginning to gnaw.

Now I wasn't homesick, or anything like that. I come from a family of ships' rats, the Stenches, of Lower Wharf Street, London. We Stenches have always been travellers. But this was my first journey and it had been a long one. And I was missing proper food. Proper fresh English food. A loaf of new-baked crusty bread smelling good enough to climb inside. Yellow cheese crumbling under my sharp teeth. Ripe pears dribbling sweet juice. Beer from the pub at the river end of Lower Wharf Street. Lying under the galley stove I closed my eyes and dreamed about the land ahead. What would we find to eat? Sugar ... whipped cream ... hazelnuts ... walnuts ... the lightly lifting layers of pastry at the edge of an apple pie ...

"Move!" interrupted Phil. "Hefties coming."

Hefties are what we rats call the humans who sail the ships for us, and any other humans on board. Fellow Travellers. F.T.s. Hefties. In any case they *are* Hefties. Heavy-footed, heavy-bodied creatures. We ships' rats aren't afraid of the Hefties. But we keep out of their way.

There was one peculiar thing about our ship though. There were female Hefties on board, or Skirts, as we say. The Skirts hated us. They screamed when they saw us. Aaaaahh! Eeeeehh! But they had their uses. They left more food lying around than male Hefties, so we could usually find a snack. They left clothes on the floor which made good temporary hiding places – just as well, given all the screaming.

Phil and I watched some Hefties working on deck, and reckoned by the jobs they were doing that we would be landing next day. It's a great feeling – the excitement of a new port. Discovering the layout of the waterfront, sniffing the smells of new streets and buildings. And there's the opportunity to meet the local ships' rats. Ships' rats live in every port, every city. We've spread to all places worth inhabiting. We are a fine adventurous race with a well-organised network of contacts and information. All of us ships' rats hoped for a good long visit on shore.

In any case we were desperate for some decent water. We'd gnawed plenty of holes in the water casks but the stuff inside was stinking.

Phil and I shared a comfortable nest in a red woollen petticoat belonging to one of the Skirts. It was kept in the bottom of a wooden box. But when we went down below to sleep, drat the woman, the box had been moved, and locked. At least it was further proof that we were about to land. We moved into a nest of shredded paper with some other mates, and tried to sleep.

The sound of the anchor chain clanking out woke me. I cleaned myself quickly. Watch out, all land-based ships' rats. I, Watkin Stench, was about to come on shore. Young, handsome, ready for anything. My fur glistened. My whiskers were soft, my tail exceptionally long. There was just the tiniest nick out of my left ear. I had fine bright eyes (or so my mother said). Perhaps I was a bit plump but at least I enjoyed my food.

We ships' rats have strict disembarkation procedures. The Scouts go ahead to make preliminary checks. There must be precise timing, due caution, name checking – that kind of thing. I moved towards the assembly point keeping to the safe fast routes we create in all ships, beneath the lining of the hold. There where the great timber frames curve like ribs to shape the hull we have gnawed holes and cleared passageways to give us access from one end of the ship to the other. Rat-height, rat-fast routes through the creaking darkness, only half a body's thickness above the deep heaving ocean.

I reached the assembly point in the stern section of the hold behind the bundles of wood stacked for the galley stove. Here Hefties had to stoop and crawl and we knew we would be unseen, uninterrupted. A quick climb up pipes and behind cabin panelling led to an exit in the carved wooden stern-work of the ship.

9

My heart beat with pride as I looked at the number of rats assembled. During a voyage we never come together, but live in small groups. Now the place seethed with eager rats. All suddenly stood quiet as our Leader, Old Gilbert, entered.

"The news is disappointing." Old Gilbert stood high above us balancing on a barrel. He seemed, as an experienced sea rat, to look beyond, to some ever-distant horizon.

"The Deck Scouts report no harbour, no wharves, no sign of a warehouse, a village, not even a road. We are at anchor in a large bay with a low distant coast. One of our Landing Scouts will of course accompany the Hefties if they take a boat ashore, and bring back reports of all he sees. As soon as disembarkation can be carried out you will receive your instructions. In the meantime you must be patient. As always be cautious. You are dismissed."

2

All that travelling, then this! I wandered off. At least I could take a look at the place where we were anchored, although going up on deck in these circumstances wasn't safe. Creeping along, darting from shadow to shadow, I climbed on top of the pens where the Hefties kept their chickens. Just as Old Gilbert had said. The shores of a wide bay shimmered in the distance, sandy-looking, with smallish trees. Other ships were anchored near us.

Moving around to the opposite side of the chicken pens I saw that the Hefties had launched a boat and were rowing towards the shore. Lucky Landing Scout chosen to go with them. One day, when I had been on many voyages, and experienced many adventures, I might be chosen as a Scout rat.

Our ship's second boat was still on deck, lashed in its place for the voyage. I edged towards it. No harm pretending; no difficulty climbing inside either. But no point being seen. I found a space under a seat next to a pair of oars – Scout Stench reporting for landing duty – and settled down for a day-dream. As good a way as I could think of for passing the time.

The boat rocked. There were heavy feet on the deck – loud voices – shouts. Horrors! Hefties! I was trapped. I had to get out – but I couldn't. I'd be seen. The boat rocked again as a Hefty climbed in. His sweaty red hands worked at the knot in a rope. I backed as far as I could under the seat, my eyes never moving from his fingers. A tug at the rope and he climbed out. He was going away – please could they all be going away – but there was a wrenching jerk and I felt the boat being lifted high into the air and swinging with an unnatural motion. The Hefties were launching the boat.

My fur stood rigid with fright. Scout Watkin Stench? No thank you! All I wanted was to be back in the hold of our ship, fast. Swinging there, above the deck and the sea, I gathered my senses. Now was my only moment to find a safe hiding place. I dashed forwards, then back, like a rat in a trap. Where – there must be a hole – come on, fool, try. The boat began to drop. I ran forward again, stumbling as the boat rocked and tilted, and found it. Near the bow a small gap in the planking beckoned, leading below to safety. As I lay, panting, in the cool darkness, I felt the boat hit the water. Hefties climbed on board. I could hear the oars being fitted into the rowlocks, Hefty voices, the scrape of boots. A trickle of cold salt water began oozing around my feet and I crept as far forward as I could go.

"Halt!" snarled a harsh voice. "Who gave you permission to board? Young fool. Get down and stay hidden."

It was Darcy, a big bold grey-coloured rat. The boat jerked through the water as the Hefties above our heads pulled on the oars.

"Where are we going?" I had to ask.

"Why do you think I am here?" grunted Darcy. "To find out. Scout duty. Now shut up and keep quiet."

Darcy was stretched up on his hind legs peering intently through a small crack. Suddenly he hopped down. "Brace yourself!" and a moment later we bumped against something.

"We've crossed over to another ship," said Darcy. "The Hefties are going on board and so will I as soon as I get the chance."

We'd left England with other ships and if this was one of them there could be friends up there.

"No you don't!" said Darcy, reading my thoughts. "You stay here. This is Scout's work only. Dangerous. Skilled."

I watched him run forward, check, then he was out in the open and gone.

I waited. I recited Ships' Rats Regulations 1 to 14. Then I crept along the same route and with extreme care poked my nose out. Not a Hefty in sight. They had all gone on board the big ship which loomed above. A rope-ladder dangled down, the end only a longish leap away.

"Why, if it isn't young Smelly himself. Wat-a-Stench, young Watkin Stench!" said a mocking voice.

Wildly I looked around, back, up, down.

"Here, young Smelly," said the voice and craning up I saw, balancing on the top of the ladder, not exactly my worst enemy but pretty close. Scuttle Butts, whose

13

family lived at the other end of Lower Wharf Street, next to the pub.

"I didn't expect to see you here, Scuttle," I said.

"I don't fancy Smelly Stenches at the end of a long journey," he cackled, leaning out on the ladder so it swung.

"Your lot are all inside drinking. The Hefties are drinking, and your Scout Darcy is drinking – we've broken our way into the best supplies of rum in this ocean, and don't think you are coming on board to share it, young Smelly Wat-a-Stench, because you are not."

For the thousandth time I cursed my parents for my name. Now here was blasted Scuttle Butts about to spread my nickname to everyone else.

Scuttle leaned out further on his rope. "Excellent grog here," he laughed, "and none for little Smelly, but plenty for our friend Darcy."

There was nothing else to do but slink back into my hiding place and wait. In fact I went to sleep – probably all the excitement sent me off – and only woke up when the slap and rush of water, and the scraping noises of the Hefties' boots made me realise we were moving again. The Hefties were shouting and singing. With all the drinking they'd done I hoped they would steer straight. I looked for Darcy watching at the peep-hole. But he wasn't there. He must be keeping watch somewhere else. I waited in my corner until I felt a thud as our boat met the side of a ship, and stopped. I waited until all sounds of Hefties faded, then went forward.

"Darcy?" No reply. He must have slipped away already to make his report without me even seeing him. Clever rats, these Scouts. I jumped for the rope-ladder dangling down the side of our ship, and was back on board.

I couldn't wait to find Phil and tell him what had happened. And I couldn't resist just mentioning to anyone I passed, "What have you been doing?"

"Nothing much."

"Oh me? Well – I've been visiting one of the other ships..."

"You! Stenchy!"

"Oh yes, just a quick trip."

I was settling down with Phil to a drink and a meal (which I needed) and a good chat when a rat raced up.

"Stench, you're wanted. Now. By Old Gilbert."

3

Old Gilbert wanted me? I'd never even dared speak to him.

"You'll be for it," said Phil looking worried. "You should never have been on that boat. Rules are rules."

I wanted to hide, to get away from the ship and come back when everyone had forgotten. But Phil said, "Come on, you're young, they shouldn't be too hard on you. I'll take you as far as the entrance."

I honestly don't know where I went or how I got there, but suddenly Phil was saying, "Knock. Good luck," and a piece of polished wood slid aside to reveal the neat luxury of Old Gilbert's private cabin.

Six senior rats sat with Old Gilbert – the Advisers. This was a Council Meeting. Even the most ignorant ships' rat knew that six Advisers were chosen on each voyage to help the Leader, and that they met in secret.

"Tell us exactly what happened." Old Gilbert didn't look at me but somehow the way he gave the order unfroze my terror and I could speak.

At the end Old Gilbert said, "Grog has always been his weakness. Thank you, young Stench. Your foolishness has had its uses," and he and the Advisers began to talk.

Useful? Me? I wasn't even being punished. I shuffled back out of the light. Who were they talking about? Then I realised. Of course. Darcy. He hadn't come back after all. The non-return of a Scout was serious. Was he captured? Killed? Now I'd given the probable solution. Darcy was no doubt at this minute lying totally drunk on the other ship.

A knock, the polished panel slid back, and a strong muscular rat hurried in. I knew who he was. Everyone did. Jaws Dawes.

"Scout Dawes reporting from the landing party. Coast dry. Undergrowth excellent. Water supplies poor. Weather hot. Food supplies: none in evidence; foraging necessary. Enemies: none sighted. Towns, roads, nil. Reconnoitre took place with Landing Scouts from three other ships. Report that all eleven vessels which departed England have arrived safely. All rats in general in good health. No reports yet received concerning departure times."

At which point I was noticed. "OUT!" bellowed Old Gilbert.

The message got around. We were stuck here, anchored in the bay, and there were still no plans to leave. Yet the Hefties weren't doing much that I could see. Every now and then a boat pulled for the shore, or crossed to one of the other ships. I suppose Scout rats went in them, but we weren't told anything. At least fresh water supplies were brought on board which was

17

a great relief after the muck we had been drinking. Hefties fished, but we only saw the bones. They cut grass for the sheep penned on deck and the smell of new green grass filled us with desire. But we couldn't leave the ship. We were anchored too far out to swim the distance in safety. Most of the Hefties and all of the Skirts stayed on board as well and they were very restless, and difficult to share quarters with.

Rumours spread about why the Hefties were here. One rat called Arthur Rope said the Hefties were looking for the king of this country who had a magnificent palace with rooms made entirely of mirrors. The floor of each room was covered in jewels which reflected in the mirrors with an overwhelming brightness, red, green, blue, purple, gold, silver. Another rat called Daly said rubbish, the Hefties were here to dig for gold, and they were just deciding where to start.

At least Phil taught me a useful skill. He'd been spending the last few weeks gnawing a hole in the chicken pens and now it was big enough to get through. There is nothing quite like the glorious gluey joy of a fresh egg as it slips down the throat. We worked at night, climbing onto the pen and spying out the egg we wanted. The whole manoeuvre was team work. I had to learn to curl my body tightly around the egg, gripping my tail in my teeth. The precious thing mustn't slip yet had to be held evenly so it didn't crack. Once it was secure I lay like a thick furry ring around the egg. Now came Phil's bit. Holding the skin at the back of my neck in his teeth he dragged me plus egg along the floor of the pen, out of the hole, and off to a place of safety where we could guzzle.

18

Phil said he had learnt the method from his mother, who had been born on a farm, whereas he was a Londoner from Deptford on the River Thames. He'd been brought up in "Old Weevil" which is what we call the huge rich-smelling food-stuffed place where the meat for the Hefties' ships is cut up and salted and put into barrels, and the bread and biscuits baked and stored in great warehouses. A place of permanent dinner, and war on rats. No wonder Phil was big with broad strong shoulders.

One evening, I think the fifth of our stay, I saw Darcy the Scout. He was in a hurry but stopped.

"You got back safely I see," he said. "I was unavoidably delayed on that ship and have just managed to return, with important news – for the Council."

He stood over me, large and bristly.

"We can all keep secrets," he said, with meaning. "So *I'll* trust *you* with one of mine. We sail tomorrow."

"Hoorah!" I whispered, to his departing back.

4

We did sail next morning, every rat of us hopeful that we were heading for somewhere interesting. The great port of Canton with ships from all over the world loading aromatic teas, casks of rhubarb, soft silks. The heady joys of Batavia with a thousand places to visit each night. The great overflowing warehouses of Calcutta stacked with ginger and indigo and casks of glorious rum. The dangers and thrills of Mozambique. I had heard the stories. But I wanted to see for myself. I felt like a coiled spring waiting for the moment of docking – whether we tied up at stone quay or wooden wharf, by Chinese junk or Arab dhow.

A high fast sea came rolling into the bay. The wind was blowing a gale. It's nothing to us rats. Get on! Get on! But, By All the Irritations, we hove to, and dropped anchor again. Every ship in the bay had been trying to leave at once. Only one did get away, I think.

So here we were, stuck again. Phil slept. He is

experienced. I fidgeted around, bothered the Skirts, nearly got my head split open for my stupidity by an old Skirt with a quick eye and a sharp knife, and finally gave in and joined Phil in the nest of paper.

Next morning I woke to the sure knowledge that we were moving again. At last. The swell seemed to have subsided a little. The ship wallowed and shuddered. We must be manoeuvring to get through the headlands into the open sea.

Suddenly a loud sharp cry went up from the Hefties. There was a splintering crunching crash. My stomach churned in terror. A great wrenching jolt shook through the ship. The Skirts were screaming. Hefties were shouting, running along the deck above. We seemed to stop, yet move with an arbitrary sickening motion. Shipwreck! Every rat for itself! But emergency procedures must first be carried through. Phil and I raced for our positions. The uproar was appalling. Confusion, yelling, and everywhere grim-faced rats running.

"We're lost!"

"Not yet!"

"We've fouled another ship!"

"The shore – we're being driven on shore!"

"Danger Level at Three." I could just hear the message passed down from the Deck Scouts through the wailing and moaning of the Skirts.

"The rocks!" gabbled a rat skidding past us in the other direction. "We're done for. We're sinking."

I could hear that sound dreaded most by every rat who has ever set foot in a ship: the crash of surf pounding on the shore, the suck and pull of cruel wave over sharp-edged, flesh-tearing hideous rocks.

The reports came through from the Deck Scouts. "Collision with ship on port bow. Still entangled. Part of stern carried away. Drifting fast towards shore. Terrain: rocks, with cliffs. Danger Level at Four."

"Danger Level Four," shouted the leader of our column.

I knew the drill. Our wreck was imminent. At Danger Level Five we must abandon ship. But the words are never used until they have to be acted on. There must not be any confusion about such a dread instruction.

I waited, almost stupid with fright. I wasn't ready. The sea is full of danger, charged with risk – but not yet. Not here! I was young – this was my first voyage. Beside me Phil stood tense. Only a muscle in his jaw kept twitching.

"Remember. Swim away from the ship as fast as you can." Phil was giving me instructions. "As she goes down she'll suck everything down with her. Grab hold of whatever comes past – rope, canvas, wood, bodies – just get hold of it and hang on. It will help. I'll try and stay with you."

As suddenly as it had begun the crisis was over. That is the way of the sea. The ships untangled from each other. We tacked and retacked in the confusion of close-packed vessels, narrow channel, looming rocks and turbulent surf. Then we were out, into the open ocean. The harsh insistent Hefty shouts stopped, the Skirts were quiet. All was normal: the repetitious sounds of sea, and wind, the creaking of timber, whistling in the ropes, the slapping of canvas. I turned in to sleep, worn out by my fright. Phil stayed up with the older rats to swap stories about near misses.

Later on, in the afternoon, Phil woke me.

"We're anchoring again. We've only come up the coast a little way and turned in between high headlands. Now we're in a sheltered cove, part of a huge bay."

The disappointment was almost unbearable.

There was the same sort of nothing on shore as last time. Everything was dry-looking – yellow-brown, with tall grey-green trees crowding between rocks. The Scouts reported that there was a smallish stream. Otherwise the same lack of roads, buildings, warehouses or anything else of interest, as before. There was one vital difference though. We were anchored in deep water yet so close to shore we could all leave ship without difficulty. Some ships were even tied up to trees – a short bridge of rope linking them to smooth trunk, and earth.

We usually ignore the Hefties once we reach port. They have their business to attend to, we ours. But I couldn't help noticing that our Hefties and Skirts seemed very excitable – staring at the land (though goodness knows what at) – some crying, others silent, some rushing around laughing and talking. I watched a group of Hefties on shore cutting down trees, then shooting guns off, drinking, waving a flag and shouting in the usual Hefty way. The other ships had come with us. I counted eleven, the number Scout Dawes had mentioned in Old Gilbert's cabin. At least when we got on shore all us rats could meet up with each other. There would be a good large number of us. But that reminded me of Scuttle Butts.

Our intelligence services are superb. Old Gilbert was able to inform us at our evening meeting that the Hefties planned to stay at this place for at least one week. Shore leave would begin next day according to the usual regulations. Every rat for itself but all rats against an enemy.

"I need not remind you of the basic rule of foraging," said Old Gilbert. "Search out the Local humans, for where there are humans there shall you find food."

The first thing I noticed once I reached land was the space. It made me feel nervous. I'm a Londoner, used to safe narrow streets, houses crowded nicely together, small rooms, dark passages, plenty of rafters, skirting boards, holes, drains, useful piles of this and that everywhere. This place had no boundaries, if you understand. No edges. I felt I could set off in any direction and just keep going, with no way of knowing why any place was different from the last. There was no shape to anything that I was familiar with. I hadn't landed in the same party as Phil and I wandered on alone, getting hungrier. What was there to eat? The air was filled with smells I couldn't interpret. There was no waft of newly baked bread – no salivating scent of sugar – no apple tree dropping ripe fruit. Not even a bag of wheat stored in some barn to get my teeth into.

"Search out the Local humans" – all very well, but where did they live? I looked for a road, a cart, a fence that could lead me on somewhere. Nothing. Useless! Only dry undergrowth that crackled and snapped with every movement. Only fine sandy earth where each footprint left its evidence, clearly marked. Only ants larger than any I'd ever seen, and spiders lurking, and the hum and buzz of countless flies and mosquitoes, and the sense of other creatures moving unseen through the same places.

I can hardly bear to tell what happened next. I was crossing some smooth brown-coloured rocks when I found one. A Local. He was standing by a tree. He looked at me. He didn't run off, or shout. He just slowly reached for a stone and – instinct grabbing me – I leapt sideways as the stone whistled down and thudded a quarter of a whisker's length from my head. The speed! The accuracy! I crouched, shocked. Almost mesmerised I watched as the Local lifted his other arm. He was holding a thick-ended heavy piece of wood. Move! Stench! I raced across the exposed surface of the rock, the Local after me. He ran with a terrible quiet speed. The shadow of the club was upon me. I saw a crack where the rock had begun to split and threw myself in, squeezing down between the sides as the split widened into a gap, and I was crouching in safety on the moist earth.

There I hid. No Hefty I knew could move like that. A Londoner wouldn't think of it. Humans tried to catch us of course, endlessly, but we knew their methods. These Locals were appallingly dangerous.

I must get back to the ship and warn the others. Moving carefully, fearfully, keeping to the under- growth, and the slower routes under the rocks, I came to the sea's edge where the water lapped large rounded boulders.

Here came the second, worst part of that first day. Climbing around the root of a tree I saw some Locals again. Nine of them – five adults, the rest children, sitting by a fire cooking a meal. Hunger drove me closer. "For where there are humans there shall you find food." Surely a scrap or two would be lying around. The smell of cooking enticed me. Was it fish? I crept nearer, alert for danger.

I shall never forget the shock of what I saw. Lying on a rock, next to big gleaming silver fish, was a ships' rat. Dead. Freshly killed. A woman reached over and picked it up by the tail.

THESE LOCALS WERE RAT EATERS! I turned and fled.

Back on board I found an Adviser who led me to Old Gilbert. I stood in his cabin for the second time, telling him the awful news.

"Thank you, Stench," said Old Gilbert. "This is serious indeed, and confirms what some of us suspected. There have been unexplained losses. You were lucky to survive." He stroked his whiskers. "We always of course run the risk of being eaten. Fricassée of rat, rat pie, grilled and peppered rat," – I shuddered, but he went on – "Hefties eat us, *but only when they are desperate for food.* Are these Locals desperate? Or are they hunters of everything that moves? If so, this is a difficult port for us rats. And there are other dangers. A kind of fox dog, reddish gold. A grey-brown cat-like creature. Our great enemy, snakes. And, most curiously," – he was going on but stopped. "Take two days' leave on ships' rations. You deserve a rest after your experiences."

Phil called in the second night. He'd heard already

28

about the dangerous Locals. The news was getting around quickly, and in any case there were others who had had experiences similar to mine – and some who had paid the price and were missing, presumed killed. The bones of our companions already lay in this land.

Phil had a few adventures of his own.

"I saw a snake, Stenchy," he said. "As long as this bunk (we were in the surgeon's cabin) and was it vicious. And I saw a huge animal with a tail like a tree trunk," – Phil began laughing – "You wouldn't believe this, Stenchy. It hopped. And each hop was as big as ... well, it could have got from one side of Lower Wharf Street to the other in a single hop. And it carried a young one sticking out of a slit in its belly."

"Yeah, traveller's tales," I said. "We all know about those. Down in the pub on a Saturday night, SRS, ships' rat special."

"No joke," said Phil. "You wait. You'll see it."

"Have you met any of the local ships' rats?" I asked eagerly.

"Not seen one," said Phil. "Not one. It's a bit strange, isn't it. I suppose they are all in the towns, not stuck out here in the wilds."

Phil and I agreed to go on shore together. I'd feel much braver with him around.

What a change! Just three days, and there were Hefties everywhere, doing what Hefties seem to do in most places, working. Carrying heavy boxes and bundles out of the ships, shifting stones, chopping down trees, building fireplaces, putting up tents. Not a Skirt in sight though. I knew all our Skirts were still on board, grumbling and fidgeting. We kept near the Hefties and we didn't see any Locals. But we did find food. The Hefties were bringing barrels and casks of food out of the ships. Of course they didn't have any building to store them in, stupidly. No cellars, no barns, or outhouses. So eating was a pretty straightforward business for us, very pleasant.

Phil and I decided we had no idea what the Hefties were doing but it didn't matter. We were quite enjoying ourselves. There were rats to meet from the other ships, news to exchange, information to pass on, gossip to catch up with.

One morning the Hefties seemed to be particularly busy and excited. We soon found out why. The Skirts were landing! There weren't all that many Skirts, not nearly enough to go round, but the Hefties looked happy to have them off the ships.

Well, that night we got our mouths into some grog. What a party. Hefties drinking, Skirts drinking. It was horribly hot, even at night, so we were very thirsty. Late in the evening me and some mates were sprawled under the flap of a tent. The ground had been cleared all around except for a really huge tree left standing in the middle. The Hefties had built a pen for some sheep, and a pig or two, at the base of the tree. We were playing a game. One of us would dash out and slip into the pen and weave around the sheep's legs. The sheep panicked and ran, banging into the sides of the pen. A bit silly really, but we liked it.

All evening thunder had rolled and grumbled and lightning flashed. CRASH. This time the thunder banged right above our heads, like a ship's cannon. A great jag of brilliant lightning lit up the camp, the ships lying out on the water, the crowding trees, the faces of wandering Hefties and Skirts, in a sudden blue-white glare; then it turned off, and all was black again. Rain was teeming down – not pattering London rain, but as if the sky was a vast full bucket turned on its side. The earth streamed with water but we didn't care, we laughed and sang, and darted out to worry the sheep. Crash! Flash! Pelting rain. Skirts were shouting, Hefties shouting, in the ships, on the land. What a party! What a night! I was charging out on my fourth or maybe fifth dash to the sheep under the tree when a mighty thundering clap, louder than all the rest, seemed to shake the ground. I skidded to a stop. At that instant a bolt of lightning came forking out of the sky into our very midst – from the vast height of the night down to the earth we stood on. It split through the huge tree from top to bottom. The tree fell with a rushing splintering crash. The topmost branches swept by me as I crouched, almost pinned along the ground.

That was enough for me. I crept off to bed.

7

You would think the Hefties might stay quiet after a night like that. But no. Next day they were even busier, and noisier. They marched along playing drums, they blew squeaky pipes and shot off their guns, they flag-waved, and cheered, and made speeches. All the Hefties and Skirts seemed to be gathered together into a great crowd. We were surprised to see how many there actually were. At least a thousand, an Adviser near us reckoned. We noticed they were divided up. One lot, with guns, we called them Redcoats, guarding the others. Another lot were standing by a table looking important. They must be the Hefty leaders. Of course we had no idea what the Hefties were saying. We ships' rats don't understand any Hefty languages. But we all agreed that this was some kind of ceremony. The weather was still terribly hot.

After watching the Hefties for a while I wandered around making the most of the chance to eat. With the

Hefties gathered in one place it was a free-for-all for us rats, and we checked out their possessions without much trouble. They really were beginning to make the place feel quite familiar. There was even a shape to it. The smell of a road or two, woodheaps and sawpits and proper cooking places. Most of the Hefties seemed to be sleeping in tents, or in shelters made of bark, old canvas, or piled-up branches. Some were sleeping in caves.

Feeling gloriously confident I crossed a clear space to a large tent. An enticing waft of food was coming from it. As usual my stomach led me. In the distance I could hear a Hefty shouting. I ran into the tent and shinned up the leg of a table (nice to find one of those!). There, laid out attractively, was a feast indeed. Bread. Wine. Cheese. Biscuits. Currants. And roast mutton. That was probably our old friends the sheep from last night. I expect they had been killed when lightning hit the tree. I shivered to think how close disaster had been. Then I chose a really tasty piece of meat.

It was a simple meal. But one of the best. Part way through I was joined by another rat. I hadn't seen him before. We ate together, annoyed only by large black buzzing flies. We had to fight them for the same mouthfuls. When we had finished we slithered off the table and moved to the back of the tent where we found a pile of boxes and papers to creep under. I felt like a good sleep. My belly was gloriously full.

Our timing was excellent. Two or three Hefties suddenly ran in and fussed over the table. They yelled and flapped at the flies, and then the tent was filled with the Hefty leaders and some of the Redcoats having their own feast, making their usual racket. The other rat and

I did our best to block out the noise, and went to sleep.

When I woke my companion had gone. I wished I'd asked his name. We seemed to share the same interests and priorities in life.

I joined Phil at the nest we'd made between two sacks. Phil was eating some kind of seed from the second sack but for once I wasn't interested.

"You know," said Phil, "well over a week has passed since the Hefties landed but they don't look like leaving yet. I can't understand what's going on."

Being such a young ships' rat I didn't have much to judge the Hefties' behaviour by. All I knew was that I wanted the excitement of visiting the famous ports I had grown up hearing about, and meeting the rats of Jamaica and Gibraltar, of Valparaiso and Trincomalee, of Vladivostock and Venice. This was all just filling in time, waiting around, although it had had its exciting moments.

A message rat raced by. "Top Level Meeting, three hours after sundown tomorrow, at Whale Stone Beach."

"A Top Leveller," said Phil. "That's something! I've never been called to one of those. Best behaviour, all rats on shore leave must attend, that sort of thing."

The evening of the meeting was hot again, with thunder rumbling around at the edge of the sky. Whenever rats gathered together that day the talk had been about the meeting. Rumours, like full sails in a good wind, grew, and sped through camp. The Hefties were about to leave for the interior to visit the king in the great city of mirrored rooms. "No, no," said others. "We sail tomorrow secretly." "I happen to know," said a rat with curiously rough fur, "that a Hefty has discovered where the gold is. Locals with two heads and four arms, so they can fight in two directions at once, own the gold and a war will start soon."

Phil and I came to the meeting place, a quiet and secluded curve of beach guarded by massive rocks, like beached whales, dark humps on the paler sand. Sentries stood on the crest of each rock, alert for danger. We rats could not be too careful. Who knew the night habits of the Locals?

We gathered according to our ships. Eleven clusters, in a great circle like the numbers on a clock. At the twelfth place waited the Leaders of each ship. Eleven wise long-travelled sea rats, watching the numbers swell. I looked for Old Gilbert and felt strangely excited and proud to see him there. I did not know any of the other Leaders but Phil pointed out a few to me.

"There's Cannonball," he said. "He's quite young; and Spy-Eye Sharp. There, that one who hobbles, that's the terrible Sever the Severed. His leg was once caught in a trap so he bit it off and escaped. That's Walnut, and over there, the old small rat, don't be fooled, that's The Hunter. The long-backed one standing by himself, he's The Marshall."

Still the rats came in, slipping over the great whale rocks in ones and twos to mingle with their shipmates. Eleven wedges of dark glistening bodies and glowing eyes, pulsating and undulating until suddenly all stood, still, as the Leader called The Hunter climbed onto the upended root of a great tree, washed silver-white by the sea and half buried in the sand.

"Fellow rats," said The Hunter. "Eleven ships have brought us to this place. Eleven Leaders have met each

35

with our Advisers, and talked. One Leader has been chosen from amongst us to take command, as long as we stay in this place. Well-travelled in the ships of many types of Hefties, long resident in the lands of several kinds of Locals, I introduce to you our supreme Leader: The Commodore."

A thin-faced rat with intelligent eyes and one front tooth missing sprang forward. The rats in a wedge two away from us cheered, proud to acknowledge the Leader of their ship.

"I shall not speak long." The Commodore's voice carried clearly across the beach, through the lapping of the outgoing tide and the distant rumble of thunder.

"There is danger in our being gathered all together. We whose business it is to guide and protect you have worked hard to discover the purpose and thus the duration of the Hefties' visit to this place. We still do not know. However, we can reveal that one ship will shortly depart, and all those who sail with Leader Cannonball will celebrate." The Commodore paused, while the rats of Cannonball's ship shouted and stamped.

"Enough. We think that more ships are planning to leave but we do not yet know which, how many, or when. Your Leaders will keep you informed concerning the cancellation of shore leave.

"As to our continued stay here. Since the Hefties brought their food on shore our supplies have been ample, and living easy. Yet – I caution care in using these supplies. We have no proof for our reasons. But I urge you to begin foraging. Discover what the land produces. Be warned again concerning the Locals; their hunting skills, their eating habits" – his voice dropped

– "are well known. Guard your lives. We know some of our enemies. There will be more as yet unknown to us.

"And here I come to a matter of vital importance. We do not know where the local ships' rats are to be found. We sorely miss their experience, and companionship. Much can be learnt, much enjoyed (cheering broke out) from the ships' rats of any port. Long live the fellowship of the rats! (Cheers.) But we have found no local ships' rats. There are many types of Inferiors here – other rat-like creatures – some large, some timid, all different. But they, of course, are of no interest to us. Is there perhaps some great danger to us ships' rats in this place? Some beast of prey, or devouring bird, or unknown disease? We do not know. But I tell you that a picked team of experienced Scouts leaves within the next two days to travel inland and make contact with the local ships' rats wherever they are."

Across the water came the sound of ships' bells striking the hour. Clang. Clang. Faint Hefty shouts could be heard from the direction of the camp, Redcoats calling out as they did every night after each ringing of the bells.

"Enjoy yourselves on your shore leave," said The Commodore. "That is your right. But remember: this is no normal anchorage. Be alert! Report anything of interest that you may see. You are dismissed."

As he finished, the thunder which had been growling all evening seemed to leap forward, menacingly, and explode over us. Rain pelted down, and we broke ranks and fled.

8

Some unknown danger to us rats? We moved cautiously, suspiciously, keeping separate from each other. But nothing happened. So we tried to forget The Commodore's words and live normally again.

The Scouts had left on their Expedition to the Interior. Phil and I discussed what they would find. Phil reckoned that we must have landed on the wrong side of this country. He was sure that it was a long thin island. The Scouts would break through the forests, leaving all the rocks and sandy ground behind, and reach the part where the Locals really lived. He reckoned the Scouts would find farms first, with fields, and sheep, horses, cows, pigs, hens, the usual things, then they would reach the city and its port, all on the opposite side. The Hefties were probably at this very moment discovering their mistake. All that we would need to do then was sail around to the right side of the island. Of course we would find the local ships' rats over there too. Phil promised there would be strange new sights for me to enjoy, and interesting new things to eat.

All rats belonging to Cannonball's ship were jubilant about leaving. "See you, somewhere, some time," they would say as they ambled past.

"Want anything at the next port?" as they sniggered with laughter. "We'll be thinking of you at the first pub we find!"

Someone made up an irritating song.

Don't rot
In this awful spot
Where the sun shines hot
And there's not a lot
To do.

There were more verses, about our obvious lack of female companionship, and other comforts. We were all glad when the order came for boarding and we could be rid of them. Even so, it was hard to see the ship sail and not feel jealous. I watched the rat I had enjoyed the feast of mutton with go on board. I'd never even found out his name. But that is the life of a ships' rat. Here today, somewhere else tomorrow − friendships made in one port dissolved as each rat follows his own journeys, each ship spreads sail for the next port.

"Come on, Stenchy," said Phil next day. "Let's have a go at foraging."

The Hefties had trodden down the ground immediately around the camp so we needed to set off into the wilds. But we cheated a bit and followed a path made by Hefties because it must lead somewhere.

What a find we made! We came to a nice little bit of cleared land where Hefties had made a garden. We weren't impressed with the variety of plants but they made a very pleasant change in our diet. Next was that best of finds, a small patch of potatoes. "It's hardly foraging," said Phil, "but it certainly tastes good."

After that we "foraged" a lot. We also took to following Hefties. Some pushed through the trees and undergrowth, hunting with guns (not all that successfully). If we found anything they'd shot we had a good tidy guzzle, leaving only bones, and the skin, which we can't bear. One of the hunting Hefties was big and powerful, quick with a stick, and we had to be very careful when he was out.

The Hefties fished a lot, and it was always worth hanging around for rejects, or gizzards. But we had to be on our guard. Locals could appear, suddenly, it seemed out of nowhere. They wanted a share of the fish. We watched as Hefties hauled in the big nets and the silver fish struggled and flapped. Sometimes the Hefties gave the Locals fish. Sometimes they fired guns over their heads, and the Locals ran off.

Locals and Hefties didn't have much to do with each other. Locals kept to the forest, and other parts of the bay. They seemed to be avoiding us visitors. Hefties generally stayed in the camp, or on the ships. Some couldn't move around much in any case because they worked with chains on their legs, and walked with a clanking, clumping noise. We always knew when Chainers were coming. Occasionally we did see Hefties wandering through the forest looking as if they were lost, or trying to go somewhere else. Stragglers, we called them. Once we found two Hefties and a Skirt crouched in a cave. The only food they had with them was old and mouldy, but anything is better than nothing, as my old Granny always said, having lived through some very hard times. So we ate what we could.

There were pictures and carvings in some of the caves. I expect the Locals had done them. They had drawn animals with their insides showing. I appreciated that. We rats know precisely the interiors of the animals we eat. Phil and I were shocked though to find a new carving of what looked very like a ships' rat. Hefties could always frighten off the Locals with their guns. But we rats couldn't be too careful. A Local was an infinitely more skilful hunter than any Hefty.

Poking around in the forest early one morning Phil and I met Scuttle Butts and two of his mates. I had been keeping out of his way.

Scuttle immediately began mocking me.

"Come on little Smelly, Wat-a-Stench, let's fight. And who is your friend? Your Grandad? Is Smelly and his Grandad lost, then?"

Phil turned and snarled.

"Don't Phil," I pleaded. "It's not worth it."

But Phil and Scuttle were circling each other, tails erect, teeth bared. I had to join in. That meant Scuttle's two mates on the other side. We hadn't a hope. When we rats fight we fight and it can be the whole way. To the death.

Phil and Scuttle kept circling. The soft brown earth, fine as powder, kicked up in little puffs. The forest was very quiet and cool. I could hear birds, their calls sounding sweet and suddenly familiar.

Scuttle's front foot skidded fractionally on a dry leaf. In that moment of hesitation Phil was in, and they were locked in combat, twisting rolling bodies, jaws grabbing for holds, sharp teeth jabbing at neck, ears, throat.

Scuttle's mates watched, crouching. One was thin and bony, the other, although heavily built, looked slower. I had to fight. Ships' rats rules laid down one-to-one combat. The bony rat looked mean. The heavy rat looked stupid.

Phil and Scuttle were heaving streaks of fur and dust, black backs, grey bellies. A spatter of blood flicked across the ground, each drop a little crater of warm red. Flies were buzzing in. I groaned. Why, oh why this terrible fight. All because of me.

"Come on," growled Scuttle's mates. "Fight. Get on with it."

Heart pounding, stomach heaving, I chose the heavy rat. I gave one last despairing look around, then began fight manoeuvres. Yet something had registered in my frightened brain, something in the flickering shadows amongst the trees.

"Move!" I hissed.

The fights broke apart. Phil and I dived one way, Scuttle and his mates the other. Between the trees, half running, half striding, came a Local. White patterns were painted on his face and chest. In one hand he held a long polished piece of wood with vicious sharp barbs cut in the top. The other hand grasped a large stone. Behind him came another Local. No white patterns. Same weapons. Then another Local. And another. They came quietly, quickly, purposefully, the light moving over their bodies like the light on the tree trunks which hemmed us in. There were fourteen of them in a long silent line and by the time they had passed, Scuttle Butts and his mates were gone.

Phil had a deep scratch across his chest.

"Just as I was winning," he said. "I'll show him Grandad! But he won't bother you again. And he'll carry a few reminders of me for the rest of his days."

9

The Scouts still hadn't returned. Every night an Adviser waited a little way along their route, watching for a sign of their arrival, ready to send a signal.

The signal came through the night after the fight. I raced to watch the expedition come in.

What a weary, bedraggled band. Rat by rat, they shuffled past. One held a stick in his mouth. A second rat gripped the end of the stick between his teeth. He stumbled, and swayed. He was being led. Something was wrong with his eyes. He could not see.

We all stood very quiet as we watched the Scout Expedition to the Interior pass by. Thin bodies. Mangy fur. I don't think all the rats who set out came back.

We didn't need a meeting. We all seemed to know the news. The Scouts had found nothing except wild forest and rough country. They had seen few Locals and no sign of the local ships' rats. They had suffered that greatest of dangers, thirst. They had reached the edges of mountains impossible to cross.

We just had to stick it out in this place until the Hefties left.

Late the next evening Phil and I saw two tough-looking Hefties moving quickly away from camp and decided to follow. We didn't have anything else to do.

The Hefties walked fast. They never stopped to hunt and they didn't visit any fields. Phil and I kept up.

"These two know where they are going," said Phil. "Here's hoping for some action at last."

The Hefties walked through the night, pausing in the grey quiet dawn to eat a quick breakfast out of a sack and were off again.

"I reckon we're heading for the bay where our ships anchored first," said Phil. "Maybe there is something there, after all."

We were getting tired. The ground was rough. We had to scramble constantly over rocks and roots. I couldn't wait to get to where we were going.

Then we both saw it. A rat. He was moving towards us, running along a fallen tree which was wedged in the branches of another. The bark hung off in shreds, brown streaks against the white blotches of the trunk.

"I don't recognise him," said Phil. "But anything is welcome in this place."

The rat stared intently at us. Something in the way he stood made me know suddenly and surely that he was not one of us. The hair down my backbone stiffened. I felt that churning in my stomach. We'd done it! Phil and I! We had found, at last, a local ships' rat. A sense of real relief came over me. Ships' rats were living here after all. There was no unknown danger to us.

We moved towards each other, stranger to stranger, visitor to local. There are well-established ways of conducting a meeting like this. It saves misunderstandings. As the senior of us two Phil went forward to talk, leaving me behind. I watched, taking in everything I could. This was an historic meeting. This is why I travelled. Here was a story to tell. I noted the details of the place – the whine of mosquitoes, the swarming sand flies, the freshness in the morning air mixed with heat, the smell of the spongy ground to our left where dark pools of water lay, the trunks of half-rotted trees criss-crossing through the coarse rushes.

By The Plague!" I heard Phil shout. He's FRENCH!"

I could have cried. All this way to meet a Frog! There were enough of them in London, or any port in the world. But here where we were hoping for so much! Our great discovery fizzled away to nothing. A silly song from my childhood kept repeating in my mind.

Watkin Stench
Hates the French,
Stick them on the table,
Pull away the bench.

By now we had lost our Hefties, but it didn't matter. I ran forward and joined Phil and the stranger on the tree trunk. The rat told us he came from a French ship anchored in the very bay where we had first stopped. There was another French ship there as well, and the rat said we'd left just as they arrived, although we hadn't seen them, being below decks. He agreed to travel back with us to our camp. When we got home and Phil and I introduced him to Old Gilbert we felt proud. Old Gilbert took him straight to The Commodore.

Our Leaders did not want us to visit the French ships' rats, although we were never given a reason. Of course some of us did. It turned out that some of our Hefties were also visiting the French Hefties although they were secretive about it. At least the French ships gave us something new to do. We became expert at finding routes between the two bays, and began to know the area much better. Now at last there was somewhere proper to go, purpose to the place, if you understand, even if it was only two ships filled with Frogs, with a long journey over swamps and rocks in between.

The rats on the French ships had been troubled by the Local humans more than us, and we exchanged information about their hunting and eating habits. But the French ships' rats had not found out any more than us about this country we were in, and they said they were equally bored, and anxious to get on. We laid bets which ships would get away first.

They won. They left with some of our rats as stowaways, including Scuttle Butts. He said the French had better grog. I didn't tell on him. I couldn't wait for his grinning face to be gone.

10

Ships are the joy of a port: all action, news, excitement. That ship, sails torn, Hefties too weak and ill to bring her in – where has she come from? What tales have the rats on board to tell? This ship, black-painted, slipping quietly at night to a private berth. What dangers from her pirate crew? That glorious man-of-war, the metal mouths of her cannon glinting, figurehead proudly painted – what battles have her rats seen? What adventures? The great enthralling *business* of the sea – it's all there, in a good port. And what did we have? Nothing. Not one ship had sailed in to join us, to relieve the boredom. Except for the French down the coast we hadn't seen a sail, for almost two months.

Imagine the excitement then, when we actually saw a ship coming up the bay towards us. At last! Fresh faces, news from somewhere.

Imagine the shock when we recognised the ship. It was Cannonball's! Back again. Why on the Seven Seas return to this place?

As the rats came on shore we serenaded them:

Welcome back
To this ghastly spot
You stupid clot
The sun's still hot ... etc. etc.

Some snapped and spat, some looked foolish. I saw the rat I'd shared the feast with actually smiling, happy, as he put his foot on shore.

"Come and eat," I said, to make friends.

He looked positively joyful.

"What I dream about," he said, "more than anything in the world, is to push my nose beneath the earth and sink my teeth into the moist crunchiness of a real live growing potato. Call me Morgan."

"Follow me," I said and led him to his heart's desire, a patch of earth cleared from the surrounding scrub like a haven to a ship in a storm. The Hefties had fenced it well but that was no problem.

The field wasn't big. I was getting slightly anxious about our potato supplies as Morgan ate like a rat starved of what he needed. But he finally stopped.

"Now tell us what's been happening," I said, and took him home to meet Phil.

Morgan told us how the Hefties had sailed to an island out in the middle of the ocean. No port, no roads, the usual story, except no Local humans either. The Hefties all got off, unloaded food, boxes of possessions, just like here, worked, chopped down trees, built huts. "Except it's not like this," said Morgan. "It's all very green and lush, and beautiful soft earth." Then, he went on, the

Hefties did a strange thing. They got back on board ship but not everybody. Some stayed behind: Redcoats, Chainers, Skirts – a few of each. The ship sailed away leaving them marooned on the island with no way of getting off.

None of us had heard anything like it. Cannonball told the rats that now they would head to a proper normal port but instead, to everyone's intense annoyance, they had found themselves back here. Morgan said the peculiar thing was that as the ship turned in between the headlands and he recognised where he was he felt strangely happy. He didn't know why. This wasn't a new port and it certainly wasn't home, but he was pleased to see the look of it again. He'd missed it.

Morgan was a useful new friend. He had a real knack for foraging. We were crazy for sugar, and he showed us how to get the honey from hollows in certain trees. He was quick at spotting birds' nests. He knew where to dig for some excellent roots which tasted different from anything I'd eaten, but good. He said he'd watched the Locals digging for them so had a go himself.

That was all fine, but I had agonisingly vivid dreams about roast beef dripping with globules of rich juicy fat, pails of creamy milk, bakehouses spilling fresh loaves from hot ovens. I dreamt of the sticky juice of pears, the smell of ripe apples, the heaven of summer strawberries – the shining red curve of each fruit, studded with yellow seeds, encasing the sweet, scented flesh.

We couldn't find any familiar fruit in this country and we wanted it. We had to scavenge for scraps from mean fireplaces and a lean-to bakehouse half open to the wind and rain. We stole from scrawny hens and nipped ahead of the determined searching pigs who would eat the hair off a dead dog and leave nothing, not even the smell.

11

Phil and I had moved into a sack filled with woollen shirts, and made a most comfortable nest. Our sack lay at the back of a pile of wooden barrels, in the corner of a roughly-built store hut, and we felt perfectly safe. We reckoned the shirts had been put in the wrong place, so no one would come looking for them.

We usually slept during the morning. No point being around when the Hefties were most active. But one morning a most terrible clattering banging woke us. Fear clutched at my stomach. Hefties were moving the barrels. They would find us!

"They mightn't disturb this corner," said Phil. "But if they do, RUN. As soon as you see the light, weave. Swerve. But keep moving. There are only two of us."

The thudding and crashing was louder now and the Hefties' voices perilously close. We crouched together, muscles tensed. Two sweaty hairy arms reached around a barrel and lifted it off the top of the pile immediately protecting us. Light – I could see light – but I couldn't run. The arms reached again and Phil leapt with a mighty leap and was gone. A great Hefty shout went up and a heavy boot kicked away the final barrel, revealing our sack in the bright blinking daylight – but I was off, racing between the Hefties' legs, weaving – thwack! A stick thudded down where I had just been but I ran, between barrels, under the butt of a rifle as it hammered to the floor, and streaked towards the door. A Hefty stood blocking the way. Swerving violently I scrambled up the crumbling mud plaster of the wall and out under the thatch, down the wall and across the open, vulnerable ground to the woodheap. Protection here, in the alley-ways of logs.

I lay stretched out, panting violently. Safe! But where was Phil? What if the Hefties had got him? I rushed through the woodheap, climbing around the sawn logs and lopped branches. He must be here.

But he wasn't. Suddenly I felt a terrible sense of foreboding. They'd got Phil. He was dead. My friend who had protected me, and helped me. I crept into the splintery hollow of a split log, too miserable to move. I was safe. But Phil was dead. I couldn't get it out of my head. I kept seeing his body stretched out, stiff. Hefties were tossing it to one side. Dogs were tearing at him. Flies circled around his corpse. I must find him and bury him. I thought about my family, and the grey fast-moving fullness of the river at the end of Lower Wharf Street, with barges, and rowing boats, and the looming hulls of ships; and searching along the muddy banks for whatever had been washed up by each tide, and getting it first; and the boom of foghorns, and the smells of buildings and streets, of humans, of London, and life. I felt most terribly homesick for everything that was familiar, and not here. I crouched aching and miserable beyond belief. Our nest was destroyed. And Phil was dead.

I heard the big drum beat out for the Hefties' main meal, in the middle of the day. Still I waited. At last the sky darkened. I heard the evening drum sound through the camp. All lights out. No more Hefties wandering about. I must begin searching. I climbed out into the open and felt suddenly older, as if a long time had passed. I was on my own now.

The camp seemed a large, strange place. I moved through it, searching from tent to bark shelter to forest edge, asking, checking. No one had seen Phil although all knew about the raid on our hut. On the other hand no one had seen his carcass either. I began to hope. Phil was a wily and experienced rat, a veteran of many a chase. But with hope came a new fear. What if he were wounded? He would need help, protection. There are always rats in any group who seek out the wounded and kill them, considering them a danger and a hindrance. I had to find Phil first.

So I searched and searched, in all the places we were used to visiting, in all the hiding places I could think of. Nothing. I was getting exhausted, and nowhere. Then Morgan came to me, and offered help.

"One idea," he said, and led me up along the headland that bounded one side of our bay, to nearly the farthest point of the camp. Tents showed in the gloom. "The hospital. This is where Hefties come when they are sick, or injured," said Morgan.

It was a place of strange smells, where I had never been. But Morgan knew it well. "An interest of mine," he said.

We peered into tents crowded with Hefties. They lay on low beds, or on the ground, rolled up in blankets. At the back of one tent there were boxes with bottles, tins with closed lids, a table, small tools, casks of wine, barrels of food. And here lay Phil. My greatest wish answered. He was curled up asleep amongst some torn strips of linen. His tail was badly bruised, and lacerated. But he was safe.

12

A war began on us rats, of shocking ferocity. Humans are our enemies, but we live with each other. On board ship we rats use the Hefties' food and water supplies, but we are tolerated. Suddenly the Hefties started protecting their food.

All storage places were gone through, all casks, barrels and sacks moved and restacked. The Hefties began building stronger food storage huts with thicker walls and locked doors. Guards marched up and down. The cooks' fires, the fishing places – everywhere Hefties were watching, quick to thwack and kill. The woodheaps were upended, the fields protected. The Hefties worked with sticks, the butts of rifles, and the few dogs they had brought with them. Fortunately they hadn't enough cats to matter.

They tried bags, and wire traps, and even laid down a few balls of poisoned food. But we Londoners were not fooled. We were used to the most famous Rat Catcher of all, the King's own Rat Catcher, Thomas Swaine, and his lethal tempting balls of sugar, flour and arsenic. We were "Swaine's Paste Veterans" – the survivors. On the other hand rats were being killed. Phil and I had been terribly lucky to escape the clearing out of our hut. My second escape from death in this place, or third if you count the near shipwreck.

We rats were not the only food takers. Hefties and Skirts were always stealing from each other. Everyone knew it was happening. So why suddenly bother so much about us? But that, Old Gilbert told us, was the sign of danger. When Hefties really start stealing food from each other, the stuff is getting scarce. A Chainer was hanged; food stealing everyone reckoned. We rats don't care what the Hefties do to each other, unless it affects us. But a hanging was quite like old times back in London. A good crowd watched, so there were plenty of pickings.

To make matters worse, food was now more difficult to find. Not so many fish were being caught. The little fields yielded very poor crops. Many seeds (not helped, I must admit, by us) never even came up. The hunters shot fewer animals so there were fewer carcasses for us to clean. The Hefties were even competing with us at foraging, learning to find birds' eggs and discovering where honey oozed in hollow trees. "It's like being in a besieged town," grumbled an old rat with a crooked tail, who had once followed an army. That was exaggerating, but the Hefties were looking thinner. If humans go hungry we rats always suffer. Some of the Hefties were ill with the diseases older rats had seen on ships. Very unpleasant. They lay at the hospital. We kept away from

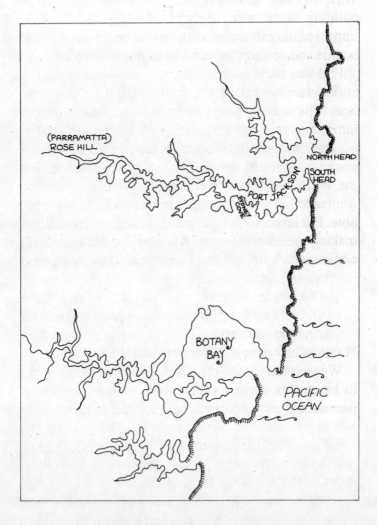

Botany Bay and Sydney Harbour

them. They stank.

At the same time the weather was becoming colder. This had one great advantage. The Hefties began building much better shelters for themselves, which improved our accommodation. Nothing like a few floor-boards and ceilings for comfort and security.

Phil was being looked after by some mates of his at the place we called The Rocks, round by the head-land. His tail was improving, and he was enjoying himself gossiping and resting. I decided to share accommodation with Morgan for a while. We were both young. I felt fit and strong. This outdoor life was suiting me, and I liked being free and independent. Also we wanted to explore. We hadn't in fact decided where, or how. But it seemed a good idea. The war on us rats was making the camp dangerous and uncomfortable. Why not see a bit more of this place while we were here?

Young rats are inquisitive,
Old rats are wise,
Old rats are careful,
And old rats survive.

"Look after yourself, Stenchy," said Phil.

We checked with our Leaders. There still didn't seem to be any movement in the ships so we were given permission, and decided to be off without delay.

13

Except it didn't quite work out like that. Darcy came up to me.

"You have been given permission to explore, so I hear. The Hefties are organising an expedition to travel inland. Several of us Scouts have decided to accompany them. On no account are you and your little friend to come. Make sure you have your walk in a very different direction."

I discussed this news with Morgan. The more we considered it the more interesting we thought it would be to go on the Hefty expedition too. Avoiding them, as well as the Scout rats, would be a real challenge.

"You are mad, Morgan," I said.

"I know. But safety in numbers!" he winked. "Think what happened to the Scout Expedition to the Interior. I'm not coming back in that state. If we stick to the Hefties we'll be fine, and we'll see more interesting things. In any case we won't go far. Only part of the way, then we'll turn back."

Even so, we nearly missed the whole expedition. As we didn't know when the Hefties planned to leave we were watching them, plus Darcy and his friends. But the very next evening Darcy turned on me.

"Haven't you gone yet? Feeling frightened? Why don't you leave exploring to those who can?"

"We go in one hour," I said. Darcy grinned.

"Why did you say that?" Morgan hissed, as Darcy sauntered off.

"Because we will *look* as if we are leaving," I said. "We'll say goodbye, and go, then hide. We'll hide down by the water, near the flagpole. We can keep a good watch on everything from there."

So we left on our expedition. Farewelled by friends, we set off across the mud flats (the tide was out), up the hill, past the big fields, and towards the open sea. Then we doubled back along the shoreline and hid.

Early next morning we watched some Hefties gathering by the landing place. The Hefty Leader arrived, with a bit of drum-banging and marching, and climbed into a boat. More Hefties got in, mostly Redcoats. They had their guns as usual, and bulging knapsacks, hung about with water canteens, hatchets, blankets, coats ...

"Plague it," I groaned. "This is it. This is the Hefty expedition to the inland. They are leaving by *boat*. Who would have believed it? Now we've missed them."

We watched in misery as the Hefties talked and laughed and checked their equipment. Suddenly one climbed out of a boat, tossed his knapsack down, and ran back up towards the camp. The knapsack lay against a rock, a bulky bulging bag of canvas and leather. One strap was undone.

"It's our only chance. Come on!" I whispered.

We sped to the rock. The Hefties were busy talking and looking at their boats. I clambered up the knapsack and squeezed in under the flap. Morgan followed. It was crowded and hot, but we were inside. We'd scarcely braced ourselves before the knapsack was jerked up. The Hefty pulled the strap down and buckled it tight, jumped in the boat, and we were off. I wondered if Darcy and his friends were hidden beneath us, in the bottom of the boat. Well, we were here too.

Cooped up in the knapsack we didn't know in which direction we were travelling. Morgan managed to wriggle down a bit, and discovered that the knapsack contained a very reasonable supply of food. As we had no idea when our next meal would be we decided to eat as much as we could while we had the chance. Morgan ate first. There wasn't much choice, only salt beef, and bread, but he did his best, then I swapped places. We couldn't solve the problem of how to get out of the knapsack. So we slept.

I woke when the boat grated to a stop, and rocked sharply as the Hefties climbed out. Instinctively I wriggled and pushed to the bottom of the knapsack. Down here there was a strong smell of leather, and Hefty feet. Feeling around I discovered a pair of shoes. Morgan appeared, pushing through some piece of clothing. We had just climbed into a shoe each when jerk – we were up in the air, bumped onto the Hefty's back, and jarred as the Hefty's feet hit the ground. One, two, one, two.

We walked and walked. Once our Hefty slipped and fell. It could have been a very nasty accident but the shoes protected us from being squashed. Sometimes the Hefty pushed through branches which slapped and snapped hard against the knapsack. I was feeling thirsty. All that salt beef. I gnawed at the leather inside the shoe for comfort. But at long last the Hefties stopped. The knapsack was flung down with an appalling thud, quite winding me. Jammed in the dark we couldn't anticipate any movements, and I felt sick.

Now Hefty hands were feeling for the buckles. I retreated as far as I could inside the shoe. If only our eating didn't show! The thought of the bag being upended, us shaken out, made my stomach turn. The Hefty put in his hands and rummaged about over our heads. Things shifted. Sharp corners prodded. We kept still. He seemed to find what he wanted. Glory be! The knapsack was pushed back on its side.

The Hefties made a racket eating and drinking. Our Hefty kept poking at his knapsack, getting things out, putting things back. Morgan and I were in a continual state of fright. At last we felt him unstrap his blanket which meant Hefty bedtime.

We crept out of the shoes ready for action. But just when we thought he had settled down the knapsack was suddenly lifted up again, then thudded onto the ground, and shaken and prodded. Morgan burrowed to one side, I squeezed myself into the other corner. As if all our previous dangers hadn't been enough. Then the Hefty dropped his great heavy head down on the knapsack, and my tail, my precious tail, was caught, held tight.

I was trapped. I could not move. I pulled and tugged,

but squashed as I was I had no leverage, no way of altering the vice-like angle in which my tail was gripped between some kind of metal box and the bony human skull. The Hefty began to snore, loud snorty regular snores.

Morgan managed to ease out of his corner.

"Go," I hissed. "You must, while you have the chance."

"No," said Morgan calmly. "He'll move. Sometime."

My tail was hurting dreadfully. The Hefty's head felt heavier. The snores vibrated through my ears. As if to underline our misery thunder began rumbling and cracking, followed by the tearing, splitting sound of lightning I was beginning to know so well.

Morgan crept up the knapsack. He worked his head out from under the flap; at least the straps had been left undone. The Hefty's thick hair caught in his whiskers. Morgan looked around. There seemed to be bodies everywhere, Hefties lying close together, crowded under the canvas of a tent. With extreme caution Morgan moved forward to the tent opening and looked out. Oh, the throat-catching smell of the night air! A camp fire burned low. In a sudden flare of flames and sparks as a log settled Morgan could see a Hefty on guard. Then the soft orange light of the fire was wiped out as another crack of thunder and jagged, branching lightning revealed trees, tents and a crouching guard in cold white outline. Rain began to fall.

Morgan came back to me.

"The sooner we are out the better," he said. "I'm going to try and make the Hefty move his head," – and he was gone.

Pinned by the tail, deep in a knapsack somewhere in the interior of an unknown country, as a storm began to rage. Adventure enough? I asked myself, through gritted teeth.

Morgan wriggled to the top of the knapsack again, checked, then crept out into the open. Our Hefty snored. Another coughed. One in the corner of the tent tossed restlessly. Mosquitoes whined in diving raids on exposed skin. Morgan slipped like a piece of black silk past the Hefty's forehead and nose, and onto the ground. He found a long curved dry leaf. Crouching on the knapsack he reached over the Hefty's forehead with the leaf, one end in his teeth, the other just brushing the Hefty's nostrils.

The Hefty shook his head. But it stayed on the knapsack, grinding even harder into my tail. Morgan tried again. A little brush, a gentle tickle. With a snort the Hefty started, lifted his head, flapped at the leaf with his hand – and I was free. Free! I felt the jolt as his head fell back on the knapsack. I tried out my numb, stiff tail. I waited for the snores to start again. Clumsily I crept to the flap of the knapsack. I smelt the rough hair of our Hefty, so close to my face, as I slid down the knapsack and onto the ground. Morgan was waiting.

We edged towards the opening of the tent, longing to be free from the smell of crowding Hefty bodies, their mumblings and snorings and jerking limbs. Beyond the tent flap I could see the sputtering flickers of the camp fire almost drowned in the rain. Let it rain! I wanted to be out!

But in the corner of the tent the restless Hefty suddenly cried out, in a dreadful moaning gasp. Instantly all the

Hefties were fumbling in the darkness, kneeling, standing, blankets thrown aside. We scuttled under the nearest blanket as light from a lantern filled the tent. We had been so near to freedom. We crouched as feet kicked aside the top part of our blanket, mercifully missing us. The Hefty in the corner continued to cry out in great pain. The others rushed around trying I suppose to do something. Morgan risked a quick peep but saw only confusion. I felt too exhausted to look, too thirsty to think.

After I cannot tell how long the groaning quietened. The lamp went out. A Hefty reclaimed the blanket we were crouched under and his feet pushed down past our bodies. We crept away, and out, into the wildness of the storm. I raised my parched mouth to the rain and tasted its joyful wetness. We ran into the comforting anonymity of the undergrowth. We had made it.

It was only now that we thought about Darcy and his friends. All very well avoiding the Hefties. But how were we to know where those Scout rats were?

I was too weary to care. We found a dry space under the roots of a great tree, and slept.

. 14 .

In the morning the sun shone clear, the air was fresh, and the world looked good. We watched the Hefties come to a slimy pool to collect water. Not our choice – we drank from the hollows and curves amongst the roots and rocks where the night's rain had collected. We fed on grass seeds, and berries from low-growing shrubs. And we watched out for Darcy and his friends. Worrying about them was taking the edge off our pleasure.

Following the Hefties' expedition turned out to be easy. Seventeen Hefties made a great deal of noise. All living things moved out of their way, so we seemed to travel against a tide of fleeing creatures. The Hefties shot at what they could see, which wasn't much, but added to the din. They slashed at the trunks of trees with their hatchets, leaving a marked trail of their passing, as if it wasn't obvious enough, what with trampled earth, bent grass and broken branches.

We came to the sea again, and reckoned it was another

part of the great bay, reaching far inland. The grass along the shore grew half as high as the Hefties. For us it was paradise. There was no risk of being seen, and endless food.

As the sun curved down the Hefties stopped by a small river and began cooking in a big pot the three scrawny birds they'd shot. We left them to it, and wandered happily, spending the night inside a hollow tree with space enough for fifty of our shipmates to rest in comfort. The rain poured down again, but we were dry.

Next day the Hefties loaded their possessions on their backs and plodded on, weary under their loads. Hefties are so clumsy. They slipped easily, and fell heavily. I have never felt so free. Every step was a discovery. We hunted, and ate, and explored. The grass was thick and high. Darcy and his friends could do as they wished. They no longer troubled us. There was room enough here for the whole eleven ship-loads of rats to spread and never even glimpse each other. Of course we watched for hawks, and other hunting birds, but the grass gave us excellent cover. The Hefties kept trying to shoot at birds. I even felt quite sorry for them as they lumbered around. They didn't seem to be enjoying themselves. Any Local humans we saw were keeping out of the Hefties' way, moving off fast like drops of water down a greasy stick.

On the morning of the fourth day the Hefties planted some seeds. Not wanting to waste good food so far from home we ate them. Then we decided to spend the day exploring on our own. We could catch up with the Hefties later.

What a day! The sun quickly dried off the silver dew. We fooled around, and lay in the warmth. We planned where we would set up home, if we lived here, each choosing more space than we ever dreamed existed back in dank crowded London. We imagined a wife; and children, grandchildren, great-great-grandchildren, whole tribes of Morgans, and Stenches, living happily under these wide skies, in these empty spaces which seemed just waiting for us ships' rats to come and inhabit them.

Something was crashing through the undergrowth. Leaping quickly onto a tree we saw a vast creature race by, a bag of grey swaying feathers on two long strong legs with a neck like a snake, and a head like a great duck. The ground shook as it pounded by.

"If that is a bird," said Morgan in a hushed voice, "just think about the EGGS!"

We thought. I imagined an egg as long as myself, rounder than I could reach, and I almost swooned with pleasure. Morgan thought about the nest it would need and his imagination could not cope with the idea of a big enough tree.

We wandered on, the image of the monster bird filling our minds. Idly I climbed up a bank of dried leaves and old fern stalks. I stopped, stunned. Below, resting in a wide shallow hollow of the same dried leaves and stalks, were eggs. Huge eggs, heavy, dark green, mysterious, the shells pitted and thick. Morgan and I moved amongst them almost in a trance. We sprawled over their bulk, we hugged their wonderful size. We counted them, again and again. Twelve eggs.

"Stop!" I yelled. "That bird! It will come back! The Hefties must have frightened it, but it will return."

We set to work immediately, trying to roll just one egg

up and out of the nest. It was far too heavy. We couldn't do it. So we worked where we were, one keeping guard, one gnawing at the thick green shell until we had a hole big enough to get our heads into. And so we feasted. Then crept away, and slept.

The Hefties, when we found them at the end of the afternoon, had camped as usual by a pool of water. The water was brown-black, edged with bright green slime, and thousands of midges clouded its surface. The trees around were loaded with parrots, settling, wheeling, perching. Their noise was so ear-splittingly loud, the Hefties had to shout to hear each other. A Hefty fired into the trees. The birds rose with a great clapping and flapping of wings, wheeled, screeching louder than ever, and settled again. We rolled on the ground laughing; then moved away, somewhere quieter.

Next day the Hefties clambered all hot and perspiring up a hill. We went up after they had finished, and saw a fine view of distant mountains.

"I wonder if those are the mountains the Scout Expedition to the Interior reached," I said.

We stood silent, thinking of the agony of their travels, and the ease of ours.

We watched the Hefties crossing a valley and beginning to climb another hill.

"Come on," said Morgan. "Let's go back to the nest. Those eggs call."

We went back the way we'd come. But though we searched and searched we could not find the nest. It was as if the whole experience had been a once-only dream. The grass, the trees, the level plain – everything looked remarkably similar. So we gave up, and wandered on.

Morgan was ahead. Suddenly he stopped, stiffening.

"Locals," he hissed. There were two men, busy by a tall almost branchless old tree.

"Let's watch," said Morgan. "We might find out about another kind of food."

One of the Locals was stuffing handfuls of dry grass into a hole in the trunk – the kind of hole we had been sleeping in at night. The other carried a little fire to the hole. A whisp of smoke coiled gently upwards from the grass, then turned to a steady, yellow flame. To our astonishment smoke began pouring out of the top of the tree, like a London chimney. As we watched a creature crept out of the smoking hole and stumbled along a branch. Two more came out. With a quick grunt one of the Locals began climbing the tree, toes fitting into notches in the trunk.

"That's one way to get your dinner", whispered Morgan.

Then we recognised the creatures. Desperately clinging to the branch, teeth bared, was Darcy. Nearer to the trunk were two other rats.

We could do nothing to help. Only watch. The smoke poured out of the tree chimney, the Local climbed higher. Darcy and his friends were doomed. Here, where we thought ourselves so safe, death was coming to our ship-mates. We are taught that it can come suddenly, when least expected, to us rats, but it was hard to watch it happen. The Local reached out for the first rat. A quick movement of his club, and he was dead.

I turned my head away. As I did I heard a shout. In an instant the Locals were gone. Off, running and disappearing amongst the trees. Silently, swiftly.

Morgan and I were dumbfounded. What – who – had saved Darcy and his mate? Then I heard it too – the unmistakable sounds of approaching Hefties.

I raced to the tree, and scrambled up the bark.

"Darcy, Darcy. Come down. Fast. Now. Follow me."

Blinking, dazed, coughing, the two rats half tumbled down the tree. Morgan and I herded them like dogs with sheep into a thick tussock of grass. Just in time. A Hefty rushed up, panting, and stared at the tree. More Hefties arrived, examining the hole, poking at the trunk, squinting up at the smoke.

Darcy told us that he and his mates had been sleeping their lunch off inside the tree when the attack happened. There was no way out of the tree except the exit they had been forced to take. These Locals worked hard for their food, we reckoned. Just as well there weren't too many of them around.

"We have to thank you, young Stench," said Darcy. "We have experienced a tragedy. A Scout rat is dead. Sturge the Purge is no more. But you and your friend saved my life, and that of Dukey's here. We won't discuss how you happened to be travelling amongst us in the first place."

So that was all right.

The Hefties were heading back home as fast as they could, following their line of marked trees. We travelled our own, shorter route.

The boats were waiting at the place they had left them. I was tempted to try hitching a ride in a knapsack again; it seemed safer, but Darcy told us he could easily get us on board. It was all a matter of timing, he said, running up the rope tying one boat to a tree on shore, and back again, to show how simple it was. As long, that is, as the Hefties' backs were turned.

The worst bit was making the actual decision to run. Judging the distance, calculating the Hefties' movements, checking the surrounding area – sky, land, water – then off out into the open, exposed, vulnerable. Darcy got Morgan and me settled into one boat then took the other with his mate.

"Always divide forces," he said. "One of us must get back to report to the Leaders."

The Hefties spent the whole day exploring the new bit of harbour they'd found. Darcy had told us we were at the very end of the bay, furthest from the ocean. But we had to stay cramped and hidden, not to mention hungry and thirsty. We couldn't see anything.

As darkness came we arrived safely back at camp. Home, at last.

15

"We will report to The Commodore in his Residence," said Darcy. "You can come too."

The Commodore lived in a real house. There were five rooms made of canvas and wood, and it belonged to the Hefties' Leader. The Commodore had access to each of the rooms – the most important being, he said as he showed us round, the dining-room.

Darcy described what the Hefties had done each day. I realised that he and the other Scouts had shadowed the Hefties, living around their camp, living off their food, and, I was sure, their rum. Darcy would never move too far from a supply of grog. That was probably why he and his friends had been so soundly asleep when they were caught by the Locals. They must have been sleeping off some heavy drinking.

Report finished, we turned to go. I hesitated. The Commodore looked at me.

"Perhaps you two young rats would like to stay for a

few moments longer," he said. "You have shown much courage, much enterprise." He motioned to Darcy. "Thank you. You have my leave to depart."

Morgan and I were alone with The Commodore.

"I think perhaps you saw rather more of the country? And what did you think of it?"

"It was beautiful," I said. "There was space – food – freedom to move where we wished. I felt ..."

"Yes?" prompted The Commodore.

"I felt all of us rats could live there. I suppose that sounds stupid. I'm a Londoner. And I'm a ships' rat. Yet – there was something which stirred in me, and Morgan here ..."

"Thank you," said The Commodore. "Now, come and eat, and you can tell me more. The Leader of the Hefties, whose house I share, has returned home from his tiring expedition to an excellent meal. However, he has been unwell, as I expect you know, so unable to do justice to it. May I offer you a splendid pie, made" – he smiled – "from the large hopping creature. It has a fine, light pastry. Then, I think, we have a slice of plum pudding, followed by a little port wine."

What a leader The Commodore is. To treat us, just ordinary young rats, like that. We were his to command, from that moment on.

16

Phil was interested in our adventures, but he was getting edgy.

"I'm ready to leave," he said. "We've been here too long. I want to get going."

As if in answer to his needs we were called to another Top Level Meeting. The beach we'd used last time by the whale stones wasn't safe any more. The Hefties roamed around too much now. They had got familiar with the place. We all had to troop out in the direction of the bay where we had first anchored, to a large area of swampy ground. We knew there would be no Hefties here and with luck no Locals.

In twos and threes we slipped along the fallen logs, jumped from tussocks of coarse grass to rafts of reeds, to half-submerged decaying trunks in the huge dark night until we reached a piece of slightly higher land which rose dry from the mud and water. We gathered in our eleven wedges. Somehow the wedges took longer to form. It was over three months now since we had been on our ships. New friendships had begun. Morgan and I separated, each to join his old shipmates. I stood with Phil again. He had travelled down with his friends from The Rocks. There were definitely fewer rats in each wedge. Some had stowed away on the French ships. But too many had died – killed, or unaccountably disappeared.

The Commodore stood waiting. The Leaders and their Advisers were grouped slightly to one side. Guard rats watched, not for Hefties, or Locals, but for the swift shadow of a night-hunting bird, the silent pounce of a prowling predator. The day had been windy, with rain. Now with darkness the air was cool but not cold. Not English cold.

"I have the news you have been waiting for."

The Commodore spoke clearly, carefully. The sounds of the swamp surrounded us, a muted throbbing, broken by the long drawn-out dismal howling of wild dogs.

"We are eleven ships. Three will leave within the week. The destination as far as we can ascertain is China. One more will leave, but as it is Cannonball's ship we do not know whether it will once again return here. The three ships are those of The Marshall, Sever the Severed and Old Gilbert."

Wild, scattered cheering broke out from my companions, and all those whose vessels had been named, mixed with groans from the rats left out.

The Commodore waited, then lifted his head. "Why have we called you together to tell you this? It is because we have been on no normal journey. We now know why the Hefties came here. They intend to stay. They build

77

their huts to live their lives out, here, in this place. They cut the trees and dig the earth because they must grow food for the future. They tend their sheep and pigs and hens so that they will breed, and increase. They plan roads and bridges for their children's use.

"Why do they wish to live here? There is no gold, no treasure, no kings to make treaties with or merchants to trade with. No ships visit with goods to load and unload. Locals live here already. We do not know why. But we are certain. The evidence is now clear. The ships which brought them will leave, and most of the Hefties and Skirts will stay behind.

"And what do we ships' rats say?" The Commodore's voice filled the night, thrilling, serious.

"There are none of our kind here. Of that we are also now certain. Shall we stay too? Generation after generation, we ships' rats have travelled from land to land. We occupy every port, we enjoy the challenge of cities, the pleasure of farms, the peace of villages. Shall we leave this place unoccupied? To very few is the opportunity ever given – to be the first, the true pioneers. Future generations will honour and revere those of us who make the choice. They will point, and say – they were the first. They were the pioneers."

He looked around, sweeping in his gaze the company of silent rats. He pointed to one group, and another, and another.

"Here, amongst you, are the pioneers of a new great company of ships' rats, the rats who chose to occupy this unknown land. We do not know its extent. We do not know if perhaps somewhere far beyond the horizon other bands of ships' rats are already in residence. But we do know that this territory is unoccupied. That the Hefties are staying. And that those of us with the will-power, the courage, the imagination, can also stay.

"We call only for volunteers. Life will not be easy, at first. Food will be short. Who knows when the next ships will arrive with supplies? But there is good, well-grassed country beyond the camp, inland, with everything we need. Space, food, security. Our explorers have returned with the news.

"Every rat belonging to the ships about to depart has the right to leave. We are sending messengers on all ships bound for London with news of our momentous decision to those at home. Reinforcements will be sent here to us immediately. As you are all aware, we lack females (a kind of quivering moan went up from the assembled rats). There are some females with us. Too few. But infant rats have been born here, and we see how they flourish and grow strong. Female rats will be sent on the first ship from London, as companions for those who are living here. Then will our happiness be complete.

"Two further points. We know that French ships have been here. Their Hefties did not stay. Their ships' rats did not stay. But will more French ships come? We are here first. We will welcome all visiting ships' rats, from whatever port. But we are the first here. We will stay first.

"Much more serious. We all know about our appalling enemies the new brown rats who have come spreading from Europe, across the southern parts of England, driving us out of our homes, killing us, destroying our families, like a plague. (A shiver of memory and misery passed through us all.) We have won in London. London belongs to the ships' rats. But in many parts of the country we have lost. One day these new rats will arrive here. We must be here first. We must be ready for them and drive them off. We must be strong enough to win.

"I leave you to talk amongst yourselves. To think, to make your own decisions."

He stepped down.

There was silence. Then sudden confused, urgent talking.

"What luck, Stenchy," said Phil. "We'll be out of this place in a week! And China! What you've been waiting for. Then I'll show you some sights!"

"Yes, Phil," I said. "But yet ..."

"By All The Fleas That Ever Bit ..." Phil stopped short. "You're not thinking of staying! Are you mad? What would I tell your parents? What, never see dear old London again? Never walk down Lower Wharf Street, never lick the froth from the beer in the pub? Never see your own dear mother?"

"No, of course," I said. "Yes, we'll be gone in a week."

We turned for camp. I walked in a daze. Suddenly Phil pushed me bodily under a log as the shadow of a night bird swooped past, the stir of air from its wings ruffling our fur. It was that close. There were such dangers in these wild places. We hurried back.

17

Phil seemed keen to keep me with him. He talked busily about China. We went on board our ship, and checked out all the changes. Things looked fresh and clean. The spaces where the Hefties and Skirts had lived were cleared out ready to take on a new cargo.

"Good old ship," said Phil. "This is where we belong. Where shall we sleep this time, eh Stenchy?"

I managed to get away and find Morgan. We didn't need to talk. We were both thinking about the same thing.

"It's easier in a way for me in Cannonball's ship," said Morgan. "There's a fifty-fifty chance we will go off somewhere like that island again, visit the marooned Hefties and come back, same as last time. It gives me longer to make up my mind."

"Yes, but it's fifty-fifty you are leaving for home as well," I said.

"I know," sighed Morgan. "Oh, why should it be *us*?

The rats on the other ships have got longer to decide. What have we got? Two days? Maybe three, or four? To choose our life? To stay here and never see family and home again, never travel, to give up the sea? Or go home, and miss this great opportunity to be in at the beginning, this great adventure, to start something entirely new?"

The rain poured down, with blustery cold winds, as if driving us away. On the third day the rats of two ships, The Marshall's and Sever's, boarded. Early on the fourth day both ships moved down the bay. I felt as if I was being dragged inexorably along, powerless to stop and make a decision – as if all the processes of leaving were picking me up and carrying me with them. The Hefty in charge of The Marshall's ship left his massive dog behind. This dog was our scourge: a rat-catcher of power and patience. It seemed another message. Go. Yet my heart felt heavy, my steps dull.

The next day The Marshall's ship left for good. We watched her sails fill. The Hefties on board waved. The Hefties and Skirts on shore waved, and some wept. It was infinitely sad to see her leave. Infinitely sad to stand on shore.

"I've made up my mind. I'm going, Morgan," I said. "I haven't the strength to stay."

"I'm going too, Stenchy. I'm taking the risk. Fifty-fifty."

We knew what it meant. When would we ever meet again? Friendships made in ports – lost, as each ship moves on, each journey begins. But this was different. We were real friends. There was so much still to do together.

"I'll come again," I said. "As soon as I get home and

I've seen everyone. I'll get the first ship leaving for here and I'll be back. Though I don't know quite why..." I felt suddenly eager. Then flat, again. "I don't know why I want to come back. It's just something about the place. I love it."

I'd said it. The thing which was hiding in me, making my steps so dull, my heart so weary, was out. I hadn't realised. Now I knew.

Morgan stared into the distance, as if into the unknown, unseen secrets of this country.

"And me," he said, quietly.

18

We were due on board an hour after sunset.

As far as I could see no rat belonging to our ship was staying behind. That couldn't be true, but there was Darcy, looking important, and Jaws Dawes and many other faces I recognised, half-friends and acquaintances. I was impressed that no one had tried to persuade us to stay. Yet that made it harder.

The first night back on ship was exciting. All bustle and action, the ritual of boarding, name checking, allocation of areas. Phil and I looked at the stores. They were nasty. Same old stuff we'd had coming out, only older, staler, and much less of it. Phil was not pleased.

"Damn place," he said. "Can't even supply us with fresh food like a proper port. Look at this. Must be all of two years old, *and* it's already been half way round the world. We'll be eating the rigging grease before we're through."

We went up on deck. There were no hens this time, so

there would be no egg gathering expeditions.

"We've a lot of space to rattle around in," said Phil. "Till the cargo comes on board. Ever thought about a nest in a chest of tea? Soft, dry, sweetly scented. We'll need the rest after the nights out in the places I'm taking you to.

> Have a rest
> In a nest
> In a chest of tea.

You wait!" Phil was really trying hard.

But I had said goodbye to Morgan, and not much could comfort me.

In the morning, early, Sever the Severed's ship which had been anchored out in the harbour hoisted sail and left. This time I was not on shore. I was on board myself. As I stood, watching, Cannonball's fast little vessel slipped her moorings and without pausing her sails filled and she sped down towards the open ocean. So fast. No time to stop. Morgan was gone.

I wished we could do the same. Leave these familiar views – the sounds of land life I was so used to – the particular smells of grass, and earth, and trees, which clutched at my chest – and go, quickly.

Instead our ship seemed glued to base, sluggish with indecision. We unmoored. We moved slowly down harbour, with no grandeur, no style. The wind had dropped. Rain fell from a dull grey flattened sky. We came to again, and anchored opposite a little rocky island sprouting a cap of trees. A boat pulled out to us. Hefties came on board. They left. The wait was interminable. I really did not know how to manage. *Let's get going*. But we stayed all night. Next day it was the same thing only worse. Once again a boat pulled down to us, and Hefties came on board, then left, disappearing up the harbour in the direction of the camp. I felt totally wretched. Phil was avoiding me. He knew I was miserable. Best to let me get over it by myself.

There was almost no wind. A hazy damp mist hung over the water so the ship seemed held in a small circle of grey sea, grey air. We raised anchor. The ship's long boat went ahead, feeling the way. Moisture dripped off the rigging like slow tears; it ran along the brasswork and jogged off, drip, drip. We anchored again, a little inside the two great headlands which guarded the entrance to the harbour. There was the sound of the open ocean beyond. Nothing happened. The mist began lifting.

After a while some of our Hefties got into the long-boat, and pulled for the harbour entrance. I hid in the rigging, gazing down at our smaller boat lolling in the water. The rope-ladder hung over the side. I remembered the time when we'd first arrived, in the first bay, and I'd gone visiting the other ship by mistake with Darcy, then come back, and climbed our rope-ladder, so frightened by my adventure, so grateful to be home. A lot had happened since then. I'd changed. Home. That's what it was all about. Where was home? I looked across the water at the land. The mist had gone. Smooth curves of yellow-brown rocks. A scoop of white sandy beach. The green-grey trees with their strips of soft bark swinging gently. I heard the calls of the birds. I smelt the strong smells of land – but of *this* land – with its sharp sweet freshness. I gazed up at the enormous width of sky. I climbed off the rigging and ran along the deck rail to the rope-ladder. For a moment I stood, checking. A rat was coming towards me, darting from shadow to shadow on the open deck. It was Phil. I ran down the ladder and leaped into the boat.

"It's no good, Phil!" I could see his dear face peering down at me over the side. "I must do this. Thank you for everything."

Then I turned away and hid under the planks in the bottom of the boat. From far above I heard a faint "good luck". Then silence.

I was happy. No doubts. I sat, quietly.

19

Several things could happen. The Hefties might come and row to the shore. But why should they? Or they might row out to the harbour entrance and check for hidden dangers, submerged rocks, like the other boat. Or I might just sit here, until the boat was hoisted finally on board ready for the open ocean. I'd most likely lost my chance. But I knew that I had properly made up my mind, and that gave me true contentment, at last, whatever should happen.

And so I waited. Then I heard the sound of Hefty voices. There were feet on the rope-ladder, the lurch of Hefty bodies stepping into the boat, the pull of oars! We were off! Somewhere!

The wait was almost unbearable. I braced myself for the toss and heave of the open sea which would mean we were between the two great headlands. Then I began to dream that we were going all the way back up the harbour to the camp. The scrape of sand on keel ended that – we hadn't been travelling long enough. The Hefties climbed out, but their voices stayed close.

I crept forward. Carefully now. Don't ruin everything at the last moment. I risked a look. The great backside of a Hefty loomed. He was sitting in the bow of our boat, smoking a pipe. Several Hefties were climbing around rocks which closed off the curve of a beach, making a little cove. The rest were digging up sand with spades and putting it into sacks. I supposed the sand was for ballast.

Escape depended on timing, but I couldn't get the moment right. The Hefty with the pipe kept looking around. The sand diggers kept wandering over, talking, and their spades were sharp edged and heavy. I could see the rock climbers prising off shellfish with knives which glinted.

There was nothing for it. I would have to bolt. I climbed out into the bright open light, and moved as stealthily as I could along the bottom of the boat, up onto a seat, and leaped. Pipe Smoker saw me, yelled, and picked up a handful of shells which scattered harmlessly as I streaked across the hard sand left by the tide, swerving in fear of hovering sea gulls, and up into the shadowy cover of the scrub. Safe!

The Hefties didn't follow. They loaded the bags of sand into the boat, pushed off and left.

I wished I could somehow signal to Phil where I was, and that I was safe. I felt bad about Phil. He would be so worried. If only he could understand. What would he say to my parents? But thinking about my family, and Lower Wharf Street, was no good. I decided to find somewhere to sleep, and work out everything tomorrow. The dark shadow of a cave showed in the rocks. I found a high, hidden ledge, and curled up.

20

In the quiet light of dawn I stood at the entrance to the cave watching the final act of our ship's departure. The air was clear. Yesterday's mists and heaviness were gone. The breeze was good enough to fill the sails, and carry the ship between the high heads and into the open sea, which signalled its presence by a heavy, green swell. I watched the two boats being hoisted up and secured. I heard the anchors come in. I knew these final preparations for a voyage. I knew the feelings in the hearts of the rats, as they sensed at last the freedom of the open sea, the release of departure, the anticipation of the port to come. I watched the ship tack, go about, manoeuvre – falter – feared for her vulnerability. Then, as the sun began to shine with the fullness of morning, she cleared the Heads, and left.

I was alone. Truly alone. How far away was the camp? I must start moving. Then it hit me. The awful unbelievable truth which had been staring me in the face all along. *I was on the wrong side*. I was on the northern shore of this huge harbour. The Hefties' camp and my companions the rats were all on the southern shore.

It was too terrible to believe. There had to be a solution. Behind me reared the great bulk of the northern headland. I decided to climb up so I could see the shape of the land. I began running, and scrambling, up rocks, through sharp scrubby undergrowth, climbing ever higher. It was further than I thought. I couldn't see anything but rocks, and tree trunks and endless bushes. I was scratched, and panting.

I stood at the top of the headland. Far out on the horizon's edge I could see the sail of our ship, a small dark mark on an empty sea. Opposite, the southern headland rose steep, golden-brown perpendicular cliffs strangely streaked with black stains. A brief sea divided us, waves running with ocean swell. It might just as well have been the whole ocean. I could not cross it. The headlands were two lips, forever parted. Behind was the great body of the harbour. It stretched so far into the distance I could only see the first layers of bays and smaller headlands. I could only guess at the complex pattern of waterways winding who knew how far, and in what directions.

I was in despair. I had left my ship but had not reached my home. I was absolutely separated from all I knew. I might as well be in another land. I could see the southern shore but I could not reach it.

I needed food. So I searched, nervously watching for whatever Locals might live on this side, for snakes, birds – and all enemies. Then, choosing a sheltered crack between two rocks up on that high headland, in view of the empty ocean, I slept.

There was nothing else to do, I decided in the morning. I must set off and, however long it took me, walk the whole northern coastline of this harbour, until I reached its innermost tip, the place Morgan and I had visited on the Hefty expedition so long ago. Then I would have to start off along the southern side of the harbour and walk until I got back to camp. I doubted if I could ever make it. It would take all my life – especially, I thought grimly, as my life would end in the attempt. I'd die. Eat or be eaten. I'd starve, or be something's meal; or lie, injured, until I starved or was finished off by a picking crow, or scavenging dog. No one would ever know. I would disappear in the wilds of this land; everyone here thinking I had left safely for home, everyone at home thinking I had stayed safely here.

These thoughts did me no good. I set off.

I'm not sure how many days it was before I gave up. I had been following the water's edge, occasionally cutting across when high land let me see the way ahead, but mostly keeping near the line of coast because the trees and undergrowth grew too thick to see any distance. Sometimes bogs and swamps forced me into detours. Sometimes the jumble of rocks rose so steep from out of the sea I was in great danger of slipping. There were Locals here, doing the same things as the Locals I already knew, and I took some comfort from that. I avoided the places where snakes slithered, or lay coiled asleep, and moved in undergrowth, hiding as far as possible from the sharp triangles of birds' beaks, the teeth of hunting animals. I grew thinner, and weary from watching and striving.

I had worked my way around a large bay, with toil and effort. Now I saw my route must follow an arm of the harbour which stretched away into the distance in the wrong direction. Yet I could see, just across the water, a pretty cove where Locals were fishing from their canoes. How much exhausting travel before I could even reach this cove? Even then I would be not much further on, still here on the northern shore, still in sight of the headlands leading to the ocean. I'd had to make the attempt. But I knew in my heart it was useless.

I turned back. I would be a castaway, a marooned rat. I would live my days on the great headland. If any ship sailed by I would see it and so keep some view of the great world outside. And there was a small chance – I dared not hope – that a boat would one day pull in at my headland and I could escape. More things were possible if I stayed in one place. Anything was better than moving on in that nightmare never-ending journey.

21

It might sound strange but I began to quite enjoy my headland. I had a routine. Food was easy enough to find. A tree grew here with sweet fruit, yellow as the silk dress one of the Skirts kept hidden in a box back in camp. I lay for hours, high on the cliffs, looking out to sea, or walked across the hump of the headland and looked up the calmer waters of the harbour towards where I knew the camp must be. It was rather like being back on board ship except there were no companions. I watched the Locals fishing, their canoes bobbing around down in the waves. I day-dreamed about a wife. At night frost whitened the ground, but the days were clear. I learned routes around the headland, and ways to get down the cliff-side to the rocks when the tide was out to scavenge for oysters and mussels. I discovered little beaches protected from the surf's reach with white shell-strewn sand, and claw-waving crabs. There were sharp-leaved shrubs, with small sweetly-scented flowers – pink, red, white. Frogs croaked in spongy hollows. Fat black lizards with orange streaks scuttled through the litter of dry leaves and old twigs. Strange little Inferiors watched from their nests, their young poking out of pouches in their bellies. The wind blew keenly here, but in sheltered places the sun warmed the flat golden rocks, and insects buzzed, and brilliant little birds darted and hovered, their long beaks dipping into flowers for the nectar.

There was a place down from the headland and along, where the land narrowed, leaving only a brief distance between the ocean and harbour. Black swans swam in a lagoon, and flocks of parrots flew out of the dark forest and across a swamp, swooping and screeching, their brilliant colours like the glass in the windows of a church I once saw back in London. But too many Locals lived there for my safety. Wherever I went I learned to watch almost out of the top of my skull for sea birds wheeling and squealing, for hovering hawks and flapping, stalking crows.

Once, for two days, great gales swept curtains of grey rain across the land. When the rain stopped I crept part way down the cliff and crouched, watching the full fast waves come crashing and splitting against the rocks. I felt the salt spray in my nose, and on my whiskers, and remembered the days before we sighted this land when we sailed at tremendous speed through unrelentingly cold, stormy oceans. How miserable the Hefties and Skirts had been, huddled below with hatches locked, vomiting, shivering, crying out.

Two days after the storm I saw what I had dreamed of seeing. A rowing boat was coming up the bay, from the direction of the camp. I could not believe my luck.

Rescued already! But instantly I was filled with anxiety. I might miss it! Where would they stop? How long? I began racing down the headland to the beach where I had landed with the Hefties. Then hesitated. No. I must keep the boat in sight. Back up to the look-out place. The boat kept coming. She was bound for me – surely. Down I started on the long steep route to the beach. I'd stay in the cave, safely hiding, until the Hefties got out of the boat. Then I'd be in, and on my way. I reached the cave. No sign of any Hefties yet. I didn't mind waiting. I stared and stared at the sea until my eyes couldn't focus.

With misery in my heart I climbed back up the hill, and gazed across at the other headland. I could just see the tiny outlines of three little Hefty bodies. I couldn't see the boat. It didn't matter.

I went back to my cave, cold, weary. My disappointment was intense. They wouldn't come here now, but I had to wait. Why should any boat come to my headland. What a fool I had been. Get used to it – I would never be saved.

Next morning very early I sat dejectedly looking at the vast empty ocean. The ball of the sun began rising over the line of the horizon smoothly, evenly, and a wedge of golden-pink light unfolded towards me across the water. Into that path of light came the small black silhouette of a ship. I shouted aloud. I, Watkin Stench, had seen it first. Not anyone down at camp, but me!

I watched and watched, as the details of the ship became clearer, and she began turning for the headlands. Who was it? The French again? A ship from England, at last? I was desperate to know. Then I groaned aloud. It was Cannonball's ship. Back already.

And Morgan would be on board. Morgan, never knowing that all the time I was here, that I'd stayed. I stood up and waved. Pathetic. I ran stumbling and scrabbling across the headland and watched as the ship sailed on up the harbour, out of sight. Then I cried.

22

Life was wretched now. The hours went by, meaninglessly. I didn't enjoy the headland any more. I felt truly marooned. I kept thinking about the rats at the camp and wondering about Morgan. What was happening? I was completely cut off, good as dead.

The third day after seeing Cannonball's ship I stayed on the ocean side of the headland. The Locals were everywhere. They had set fire to the scrub and it burned hot and steady, grey-white smoke billowing up. Curse them. The fire destroyed my food supplies. I would be forced to move. So what!

Dispirited, lacking the desire to do anything, I worked my way around the edge of the headland, skirting the blackened ground. I was tired of smoke, tired of the whole place. I thought of the cave at the beach where I'd landed. I would sit in the cave, and remember what I had lost.

No flames licked at the scrub on this side. Pushing through the undergrowth I reached the beach. But as I neared the cave something which we rats call our survival sense made me check and change my approach route. I peered in. The final straw. An old Local, a man, was lying in the cave. In *my* cave. A small girl Local squatted beside him.

I turned away. I didn't know where to go. Fire on the top, Locals everywhere. I sat glumly in a clump of fern, forgetting time, trying not to think.

I heard a noise. It couldn't be. I listened with every hair on my body quivering. And I heard it again. The long distinctive squeak of oars in rowlocks. I dashed to the edge of the scrub and looked out.

And there it was. *A boat*. And I'd never even seen it coming. I could so easily have missed it. Almost mesmerised I watched the boat run ashore, the Hefties climb out, throw their knapsacks over their backs, pick up their guns and hatchets, and walk off. An expedition! I could show them this place. But I wasn't moving. No way! As soon as they'd gone, noisily pushing their way up the hillside, I was out, and on the boat. Oh joy!

There was food on that boat, wrapped up against the flies. Cold pie, the meat nicely nestling between pastry. Plum pudding. Wine. I sniffed the glorious scents. My stomach murmured its pleasure. My throat tickled in anticipation. A shadow fell on the boat.

Horrors. I'd forgotten the Locals in the cave. Hide! Hide! I dived under a seat and wormed in amongst some bundled rope. No safety from reaching hands but I was cornered and I'd fight.

It wasn't the old man, but the small girl child. She stood staring at the boat. She stared, then gently, carefully began touching each thing, picking each object up, turning it round, putting it back in exactly the same place. She was the quietest human being I'd ever heard. Somehow, under the seat, I felt quite safe from her. Then she went, feet hardly sounding on the wet sand.

I stayed in the boat, moving to a safer hiding place.

When the Hefties came back they got out their food. They dug holes in the sand and sank their bottles of wine in the cool dampness. Phil, I remembered, always called wine "Oh be Joyful". Well, I was joyful enough. One of the Hefties walked along the beach towards the cave. I wondered if the Locals were still there. They were! The Hefty raced back to his companions and off they all went, running. What a noise. I could hear the girl child wailing and crying in fright. One Hefty picked up his gun and shot a couple of birds and took them into the cave. I expect they were a present of food for the old man. He could eat birds – I tucked into a bit of pie, and had a quick gulp of pudding. I considered sinking my teeth into the cork of the wine and taking a swig. Too risky. Then I was back in hiding in the bottom of the boat. The Hefties returned, so jolly they didn't notice any missing food. They ate, drank, piled everything into the boat, and we were off. Without a doubt, I was on my way home.

Except not quite. Eager, bursting with anticipation, I felt our boat make a familiar grating bump, followed by a bobbing motion. We were tying up to a ship. The Hefties climbed out and I got a chance to look. There, just across the water, were the well-remembered shapes of the camp – the tents amongst the trees, buildings half finished, tree stumps, pigs, hens, Hefties, Skirts. We were tied up to a ship out in the harbour – I squinted up and saw it was The Hunter's. These Hefties must be some of those who lived in comfort in their cabins.

Boarding a ship not one's own carried severe penalties – unless you were a Scout, of course. But I didn't belong to any ship now. I decided I still could not take the risk, not after everything I'd been through. So I stayed in the boat hoping that sometime, before too long, before I got too desperately hungry and thirsty, someone would come and row to shore.

My release came the very next morning. Hefties lowered themselves into the boat, and in no time we were tying up.

I was filled with so many emotions as I stepped on to land. Joy, relief, strangeness. I felt as if I had been away on a long voyage. Yet this was not at all like the coming home to Lower Wharf Street I often dreamed about, at night, while I slept. Then, in my dreams, I experienced every detail – the slow journey up the river, the crowding in of the great city, the first sight of our street, the meeting with each dear member of my family. But here, I felt uncertain. I didn't quite know where I belonged.

I looked up at the flagpole. The flag was fluttering, just as it had every day since our first landing.

Rats stared at me. I said nothing. I had one need, to find Morgan. It was morning, a dangerous time to be out.

I slipped across the stream, past the Skirts washing their clothes, hid under a hut as a line of Chainers shuffled by, shovels on shoulders, got past Hefties hauling wood, and carrying stones, past more Hefties wheeling barrows of manure, or sitting on tree stumps smoking their pipes, up and on to the hospital. I had a feeling I would discover Morgan here. There was always action at the hospital and Morgan liked to watch. And sure enough, we found each other.

Morgan's astonishment was pure joy.

"Stenchy! What in the...Where did you...Has a ship arrived? How did you get here? Where have you been?" The questions rushed out. "We must go somewhere private. I want to know everything." He led me behind the tents, past a garden guarded by Hefties, and on up to the rocky point of the headland, where Redcoats had made a little building. There were telescopes inside. "No one comes here at this time," said Morgan.

We sat on a telescope and I talked, and Morgan listened, and I told him more, and he was impressed, and I told him everything, and he was amazed. What happiness.

We got down onto the ground and worked out a map of where I'd been, and then we added all our travels in this place. They were pretty extensive.

Later, in the evening, I sought permission to report to The Commodore.

The Commodore was examining the foundations of his new house – the house being built of brick for the Hefties' Leader.

"We know that four more ships are preparing to leave," said The Commodore. "You will join those of us who have made the decision. The Stayers. You are most welcome, Stench. I am very glad to see you. Very glad indeed."

We Stayers kept together now. We had a Leader called Major Zachariah. I liked him. He was fat. He knew how to feed well, and that knowledge was always useful.

One morning just as the sky broke into dawn we were woken by the most tremendous racket. The ships in the harbour were firing their guns – crash – boom – each explosion echoing around the rocks and mixing into the next. We rushed from our nests and hiding places. What was happening? Was a war beginning? Frightened birds rose screeching. Hefty babies started wailing. But, after all, it was just another of the Hefty celebrations. They spent the day marching back and forth, waving flags, shouting, drinking grog. The guns fired again in the middle of the day, on the ships and on land.

As darkness came monster bonfires were lit and Hefties and Skirts danced and sang in the red flamelight, far into the night. Zac called us Stayers together and we had our own celebration. We drank to our decision, and to our new land, and to our Commodore. We sang songs about home, and called for toasts to absent friends. We fooled around in the red glow of the Hefties' bonfires, and the warmth heated our cold bodies. I thought about that first party in the thunder and rain when the weather was so suffocatingly hot, and the lightning struck the giant tree in the middle of the new camp. Now the flames lit up the square shapes of huts, the comforting bulk of chimneys, the straight lines of fences.

Some of us got very drunk. Two rats fell off a log which the Hefties had put across the stream to make a bridge. They drowned, too drunk to save themselves. That was a waste. We couldn't spare anyone.

The Hefties were getting hungrier. Their food supplies were poor. I already knew that, having seen the stores on board Old Gilbert's ship. The flour was a horrible yellow colour and tasted sour. The meat was old salted pork, or beef like bits of grey leather. The rice and the oatmeal heaved with weevils (not that we cared, weevils were food as well). Our favourite ships' biscuits were either rock hard, or disgustingly soft and musty. Either way they crawled with beetles. The cheese was alive with mites. Currants and sago and goodies like that were finished. There were barrels of peas, but we hated them. Any butter was rancid. The rum was still good – when we could get it. Hefties were digging out a hole in the ground for a cellar, and the gloomy amongst us were sure it was for the rum. "Locks and keys to break through once that's finished," said Zac. The days of our seed sacks seemed like a distant party.

Many of the Hefties were sick with the sea disease. They lay with twisted limbs, their lips black, their gums bleeding, their skin erupting with boils. Morgan told me Cannonball's ship had gone to an island to catch fresh turtles for food. But they had not found one.

The crops grew poorly. We were partly to blame, of course. We stole; but so did the Hefties. It was becoming survival of the fastest. The Hefties ate everything they could get their hands on. They trapped the large scaly lizards which clung, staring, to the trunks of trees. They roasted snakes. They shot at birds until scarcely a call sounded around camp. They killed and ate all small creatures they could including the Inferiors. The large hopping animals were rarely seen now, and there were few fish in the sea. Hefties searched through the woods eating berries, pulling leaves off bushes, chewing the clear golden gum which welled out of the bark of certain trees. They sat over their cooking fires catching the drops of fat which fell from their meat in saucers of rice. We rats are the scavengers. But the humans were now doing the scavenging and leaving us less to find. We feared that they would soon be hungry enough to try adding us to their diet. The days were wintry – cold and wet. Always a difficult time for us rats. Food is scarce in winter.

Yet I didn't worry. I knew that beyond the place where the Hefties lived there was good country where we could survive. Around the camp the Hefties had cut down trees, uprooted bushes, trampled down the wild grasses, frightened and killed off the animals. Go where the Hefties weren't. Then we would find all we needed. Morgan and I often talked about this. We wanted to go to the land we had explored, to the head of the harbour. We could live there until the ships arrived from England with all the supplies we were waiting for.

The harsh conditions meant that the decision whether to stay as pioneers or go with the ships was very tough. But most rats had made up their minds by now. There were rats who thought that despite all the risks they could do better for themselves and their families in this new land. Their children were growing up, and calling this place home. Some rats were sending back messages for wives, brothers, sisters, or parents to join them. There were rats who chose to keep away from things at home they preferred to forget – rats who were guilty or sad. And there were rats like Morgan and me who were stirred by adventure; who planned to be among the pioneers; who were growing to love this land. We Stayers were a small but good-sized band.

The test came when we watched four of our ships leave. So many rats climbed on board, eager, full of anticipation, boasting about what they would do at the ports to come. We braced ourselves, and waved farewell.

Everywhere felt so empty after they left. We were used to seeing the ships anchored off shore. Still, fewer rats and fewer Hefties meant fewer mouths. Cannonball's ship set off again, but Morgan had no problem with that.

"She'll come bouncing back here, you watch," he said, and sure enough, back she came about a month later.

The Hefties were working hard trying to make a town. Bits stuck up as if spilt out of a bag – a brick building or two, a row of wooden houses, a few roads and fences, the thatched storage huts, a red-fired forge ringing with the sound of hammer on metal, a quarry where stone was cut. Spring had started which made things look more cheerful.

Then The Hunter's ship left. That was hard to take because she was a ship-of-war, and her guns had been comforting so far from home. Her Hefties looked thin and gaunt. Rumours spread that she was going on a long difficult journey, and few dry eyes saw her go. Spy-Eye Sharp's ship left next day. The supplies taken on board were meagre. But the rats who crowded on board were certain that relief was not far away.

"The first port," they said, "then food. We know it's coming. You lot – you Stayers – what have you got to hope for?"

But Morgan and I were not bothered. We were looking forward to our great move. The Commodore had called the last of the meetings. This time we walked out beyond the Brickfields, past the kilns, and the rows of drying bricks, and the little huts where the brickmakers lay sleeping. The sky was softly black, heavy with a brilliance of stars quite unknown in England.

We stood in groups of friends and acquaintances, no longer separated according to ships.

"We face difficult days," said The Commodore. He looked older, and weary. "We will divide our forces, until the ships arrive from England with the supplies which we know will come, must come, soon. Some of us will stay here, at our headquarters. Here we have our homes, we know the routes, we can keep contact with the Hefties, and watch the harbour. Some of us will move inland to the new country at the head of this great bay.

There conditions are good and foraging will be easier. I will continue in command here. Major Zachariah will lead the band inland. The younger rats will go with him, and those without families."

We didn't know exactly when or how we could make the journey inland. The route was long and largely unknown. It was sure to be rough and dangerous. So we waited. Then we had a real piece of luck. We discovered that the Hefties were doing the same thing as us. They were going to make a second camp at the head of the bay at the place we had chosen. Now we could travel up by boat, in comfort, amongst all their possessions.

We left on a day of hail, rain, lightning, thunder – you name it, the day hurled down misery. The Hefties moaned and grumbled. We didn't mind. We were true pioneers. Let the weather do its worst. Morgan and I were tucked inside a roll of tenting. New canvas tastes very pleasant – it's the starch in it – so we had a good chew. In any case the canvas would make excellent nest lining. We thought about the morning when we had crept so bravely inside the Hefty's knapsack and set off into the unknown on our expedition. This time we knew where we were going. The country we had discovered awaited us.

. 24 .

I move forward, nineteen long months. Months of hard living, of dangers and adventures, and of hunger. We rats at the new settlement managed much better than those left at the main camp, where Hefties driven by hunger hunted our companions, and ate any they caught.

Despair set in. No sail ever rose over the horizon in the endlessly empty ocean. No ship worked up the harbour. In the centre of our beings we were afraid: afraid that we had been forgotten – that our mates had abandoned us. Had any of the ships carrying our messages ever even reached London? We would rot here. Pioneers of nothing.

But all this is another story. For a ship – at long, achingly last – has arrived, from England. The first to come since we landed in this country. Morgan and I hear the joyful news up at the new settlement, and hurry back to the main camp as fast as possible. This time we make the journey by land. A track now winds along the edge of the bay. Morgan and I achieve a remarkably daring leap into the rolled up blanket of a Hefty riding back by horse. I will not give the details of our journey – but we arrived at the camp with eager excitement. What changes! We are amazed at the Hefties' work. Wharves – roads – storehouses – cottages with gardens.

But our eyes are on the marvellous sight of the wonderful ship anchored out in the harbour. The Hefties seem overjoyed. There are Skirts everywhere. The ship has brought nothing but Skirts! There never were enough, of course. Now the Hefties will be happy.

We go to visit The Commodore. He is settled in his fine new brick house. He kindly shows us around, especially upstairs where the Hefty Leader sleeps. We admire the real glass windows.

"Comfort at last," says The Commodore. "Warm in winter, cool in summer, and dry when it rains."

He questions us about conditions at the new settlement, tells us the news of the camp, and asks us to wait. And then he brings in the best surprise I ever had in my life. My sister Dolores. But I only have eyes for her friend. She is the most beautiful creature I have ever seen. Her fur is so soft, her eyes so gentle, her tail so exquisitely long, and neat. Her name is perfect. Jenny.

I am in love. Morgan seems equally amazed by the sight of my sister. And who has sent them? Phil. A true friend. There is news, plenty of news, from my family, from good old Lower Wharf Street, and news for Morgan too. But the best part of all is that Phil is now married, and who to? To my oldest sister Vanilla. He and Vanilla are living with my parents and they have plenty of children, including a little Watkin. I am quite overwhelmed.

Morgan and I invite Dolores and Jenny to tour the neighbourhood. We tell them about our adventures, and show them where everything happened. They are amazed, and very impressed.

While we are away a second ship arrives. She is loaded full up with stores and supplies. At last! So much happening after so long a gap. We come back to Hefty feasting and celebration.

The Commodore gives a magnificent party in his house. The place is crowded but we don't mind. What food! Goodies we have not seen for over two years. It's guzzle time. There are pies bulging with fruit, the layers of pastry almost floating off the top. There is freshly baked bread, crusty outside, bouncy yielding inside. Cheeses – lemon-coloured cheese to gnaw, blue-veined sharp-tasting crumbly cheeses, soft yellow cheeses. Plum-cakes – sugar – small black wrinkled currants – red jellies; wine, brandy, port.

The Commodore climbs up onto a box and makes a speech.

"Fellow rats, newcomers – and our noble band, the Stayers. The time of hardship is over. We rejoice in the supplies and provisions so badly needed. We welcome the new arrivals. I toast the bravery and endurance of the Stayers! I toast those who will never be forgotten – the Pioneers!

"And now it is my pleasure to announce the names of ten new Scout rats. Our numbers have increased. We need the knowledge and assistance of the courageous and experienced, of those who know what it takes to survive here. I promote the following to the rank of

Scout:
    The Brewer
    Jeremiah Firkin
    Bones Jones..."
I know he will call Morgan. And he does. I am so
happy for him. He deserves it. But please, please can it
be me too. I wait, tense.
    "Ben Richards
    The Ruffler
    Cupper Scamp
    Watkin Stench..."
I've done it! Watkin Stench! I am so proud I don't
even hear the rest of the names.

After the party I take Jenny to see the moon rise over
the harbour. The night is cold but the moon is a great
thick, cream-coloured ball in a beautiful black sky
glowing with stars. Morgan takes Dolores for a walk
along the headland. I ask Jenny to marry me and she says
yes. Dolores asks Morgan and he agrees. So we have our
wives.

The very next day the shouts go up again from the
Hefties, and we know what they mean. We race for the
harbour. A sail! A sail! We stand and watch the big ship,
water-worn and weary, come up the bay. This is the first
of the ships from England Morgan and I have actually
seen arrive. The anchor is dropped. Hefties go out in
their boats to board. Their boats come back. We wait for
that proud moment: the arrival of the Landing Scouts
from off the new ships. Scout rats to *us*. To our port. *We*
will show *them* the way around. *We* are the locals.

Then two more ships come in. They wait out in the
bay. Early in the morning they are warped right in, close

to the wharf. The new Hefties begin coming on shore. But Morgan and I take no notice. We are here for something else.

And then they come. The rats. Streaming off the ships, grey-black backs glistening – moving ropes of rats, plankfuls of rats. We have done it! Now we are truly on our way. This is our country, and we are colonising it. We are hundreds. The hundreds will soon be thousands, and the thousands, millions, taking over all the places which suit us.

Ships' rats! Hoorah! Forever!

Historical Note

Eleven ships carried over a thousand men and women from England to Australia in January 1788 to begin a settlement. Everything on board the ships was listed: convicts, soldiers, officials, horses, sheep, chickens, cattle, goats, pigs, turkeys. But no one listed the rats. All ships contained the black or ships' rats and they were taken for granted.

Thomas Swaine, the King's Rat Catcher, published a list of the rats he had destroyed on His Majesty's ships--of-war, from 1775 to 1779: *Warspite,* 146 rats; *Marlborough,* 342; *Dragon,* 146; *Essex,* 127. The list goes on. Seventy-nine ships, approximately 18,000 rats. But there were always more, tucked in the hold of each departing ship.

Watkin Stench travelled to Australia on board the convict transport *Charlotte. Charlotte* carried 20 female and 88 male convicts, 2 children, 44 marines (soldiers) with 6 wives and one child, and 30 seamen.

Everything that happened to the humans in Watkin's Journal really did happen. The ceremonies, the expeditions, the departures of the ships, the celebrations, the meetings with the Aborigines who lived around the shores of Sydney Harbour and Botany Bay. Convicts and soldiers laboured to build shelters, to cut down trees and clear the ground so that vital crops could be planted. The sequence of dates is correct, even the weather is as it really happened.

The strangers found it difficult to live in this unfamiliar land. Crops did not grow. No ships arrived from England, and the little settlement came close to starvation. Home was three quarters of a year's sailing time away. Men and women felt desperately isolated. Then, at long last, five ships arrived, in June 1790, with food, badly needed supplies, more convicts, more soldiers. And more rats.

Several of the Englishmen who came to Sydney Cove in 1788 wrote journals describing their experiences. One of the best was written by a young officer in the Marines, Captain Watkin Tench. "The rats," noted Tench, "soon after our landing, became not only numerous but formidable, from the destruction they occasioned in the stores."

Tench was one of The Hefties on board the *Charlotte*. Now, in his journal, Watkin Stench tells the story of the rats.

Departures and arrivals of all ships in The Journal of Watkin Stench

13 May 1787, 11 ships depart from Portsmouth, England under the command of Captain Arthur Phillip RN.

The Fleet consists of:

2 Royal Naval vessels

HMS SIRIUS, Captain John Hunter RN

HMS SUPPLY, Commander, Lieut. Henry Ball RN

6 convict transports

ALEXANDER, Master, Captain Duncan Sinclair

LADY PENRHYN, Master, Captain William Sever

CHARLOTTE, Master, Captain Thomas Gilbert

SCARBOROUGH, Master, Captain John Marshall

FRIENDSHIP, Master, Captain Francis Walton

PRINCE OF WALES, Master, Captain John Mason

3 storeships

FISHBURN, Master, Captain Robert Brown

GOLDEN GROVE, Master, Captain Sharp

BORROWDALE, Master, Captain Readthon Hobson

18 January 1788, the ships begin arriving in Botany Bay, New South Wales

26 January, the fleet leaves for Sydney Cove, Port Jackson as two French ships arrive on an exploring expedition

15 February, HMS SUPPLY departs for Norfolk Island in the Pacific

11 March, French ships depart from Botany Bay

20 March, HMS SUPPLY returns from Norfolk Island

5 May, LADY PENRHYN departs
6 May, SCARBOROUGH departs
6 May, HMS SUPPLY departs for Lord Howe Island
8 May, CHARLOTTE departs
25 May, HMS SUPPLY returns from Lord Howe Island
14 July, ALEXANDER, BORROWDALE, PRINCE OF WALES, FRIENDSHIP depart
17 July, HMS SUPPLY departs for Norfolk Island
26 August, HMS SUPPLY returns from Norfolk Island
2 October, HMS SIRIUS departs for Cape of Good Hope
3 October, GOLDEN GROVE departs for Norfolk Island
10 November, GOLDEN GROVE returns from Norfolk Island
19 November, GOLDEN GROVE and FISHBURN depart

3 June 1790, LADY JULIANA, *convict transport,* arrives
20 June, JUSTINIAN, *storeship,* arrives
26 June, SURPRISE, *convict transport,* arrives
28 June, NEPTUNE and SCARBOROUGH, *convict transports,* arrive